the Iron Bodkin

The Iron Bodkin

The Sardonyx Trilogy
~Book One~

Amy Allgeyer Cook

Cover by Heidi Schmidt

For Mom & Dad.
-AAC

Chapter One

The boy sat still as a statue, crammed into the dusty storefront display between the scrying mirrors and powdered cat entrails. His long, brown hair was held back with a twist-tie and his dark eyes worriedly scanned the street. The sign in his hands read:

For Rent--
11-year old Boy
Down payment required

Two people had already stopped, but neither seemed to need an eleven-year old boy. Actually, the lady in the olive green coat looked a bit shocked as she hobbled away, but a promising prospect was approaching now. Lux held up his sign. She smiled and came closer.

That's right, he thought. *Everybody needs an eleven-year old! If she makes the payment right away, I might still have time to--*

"Lux!" cried a voice behind him. "Get out of the window display and throw away that ridiculous sign! You are not going to sell yourself."

"Not sell," said Lux. "Rent. The sign says 'For Rent'." He turned back to the window and saw the woman walking away. "Mom! She's leaving!"

Lux jumped down from his stool and caught his t-shirt on the shelf. Mirrors crashed against the glass and clouds of powdered catgut filled the storefront.

"Oh, Lux. Not again!" His mother sighed as she dropped a cardboard box to the floor. "That's the third time this week!"

"Sorry." He picked up a book and fanned the dust away. "I'll clean it up. I'll make it even better, if you'll let me have some hellebore."

His mom tugged open a box of Chinese health balls. With her dark hair hanging in a lopsided ponytail, she looked like an older version of Lux.

"Hellebore?" she said. "Absolutely not."

"Why not?" said Lux.

His mom frowned. "You mean, other than the fact that it's poisonous? What kind of mother lets her son have toxic herbs?"

Lux raised his eyebrows. "A really cool one?"

His mom smirked. "Too bad for you, I was never cool. And I won't sell you any either, if that's why you're trying to make money." She walked to the back of the store and into the supply room.

Magic supplies of every kind filled the long, narrow shop. Books, stones, herbs, jewelry, robes... *If you need it,* went the motto, *rest assured you will find it at Pickingill's Magical Notions.* Not the catchiest of slogans, Lux had to admit, but why mess with something that had worked well for one-hundred and eighty years?

His mom returned with another box. "If you tell me what potion you're working on, I'd be happy to give you an alternative version."

"You mean a kiddie cocktail." Lux rolled his eyes. "No way. I'm not a baby! I only have four years before I apply to the Institute for Magical Crafts. How am I going to be ready for the ETAT if I never get real ingredients?" ETAT stood for the Elixirs and Tonics Aptitude Test. Lux dreamed of making a perfect score on the ETAT and becoming an International Class Magic Chemist.

"You'll get real ingredients when you're old enough to be responsible with them," said a voice.

Lux jumped as his great-aunt, Sophia Pickingill, appeared next to him.

"Hellebore, for Brighid's sake!" Her eyebrows drew together. "Could you have asked for anything more deadly?"

"Uh, yeah," said Lux. "Wolf's Bane. Hemlock. Wormwood, Bella Donna—"

"My, my! You have been studying! I'm impressed." She peered at him over her spectacles. "Impressed, but unswayed. You will have access to

3

those herbs when your parents deem it appropriate. And not before. Now, how about putting that mirror display back together?"

"Yes, Aunt Sophia." Lux didn't argue. Whatever Aunt Sophia said became law. Lux loved her despite her strictness. She never talked down to him, and she baked excellent pie.

"Now, where is your sister?" said Aunt Sophia. "I want to congratulate her on her straight A's."

Lux's stomach clenched. *I can't let them find Umbra. Not yet.* "Um, I'm not sure."

Aunt Sophia regarded him over her glasses. "How did you do on your report card?"

"Please don't ask," said Lux.

"Three C's and two D's," his mother said. "Honey, if you applied yourself more, you'd do as well as Umbra."

Lux groaned.

"You just don't try hard enough," she said, for the thirty-thousandth time. "Your father didn't get to be advisor to the President by slacking off. You're a Pickingill-St. Clare. People expect great things from you. You can't disappoint them."

Lux dug the toe of his shoe into a ragged seam in the carpet. *Can't disappoint you, you mean.*

Aunt Sophia clapped her hands. "Well, I'll just have to congratulate Umbra later."

Sure. Like she doesn't get straight A's every time.

Lux went to the front window and began cleaning up the mirrors. His aunt handed him a box for the shards of glass. "Aunt Sophia, how come I'm always messing stuff up?"

"It's all a part of learning." She smiled. "You'll outgrow it someday, but you'll be the better for all those mistakes. I promise."

"If you say so. I'm sick of doing stuff wrong." *Especially stuff like this morning.*

Unknown to his mother and aunt, Umbra was sitting in the basement, completely invisible. Lux didn't know how it happened. He hadn't been working on invisibility potions. He'd been working on a tonic to make peas taste like strawberries, but he tried the tonic himself so many times that he couldn't taste anything.

So he asked Umbra to try it. She popped a couple peas in her mouth and made a face that said he had not been successful. Then, she turned back to the doll she had been dressing, picked up a little bundle of cloth and faded from view.

Lux was horrified. Invisibility was a Class Five, Arrest-Warrant Skill. And if Umbra went to jail, he'd be grounded for life.

He had searched all morning for a remedy but found only one recipe and it contained hellebore.

Aunt Sophia studied Lux as he picked up the broken glass. "Why do you need hellebore? What are you working on?"

"Oh, uh…"

A crash echoed through the store. Lux turned and saw his mom frozen over a cardboard box. Silver balls rolled in every direction, tinkling like bells.

"Cerri?" said Aunt Sophia. "What's wrong?"

Lux ran to his mom.

"Inquisitors are coming," she said, relying on the Pickingill gift of clairvoyance.

"Ah." Aunt Sophia clucked her tongue. "I wondered how long it would be."

Lux's stomach clutched. *Inquisitors? Now? They usually send an announcement.*

Inquisitors inspected the store once a month to make sure Cerri didn't sell anything restricted or illegal.

Has it been a month already? This is bad. Really bad. If they find Umbra...

Aunt Sophia and his mother gathered up the loose balls. Lux hurried toward the storeroom to warn his sister. She needed to stay hidden. Plus, he'd left all his grimoires on the work table, even the banned out-of-print ones.

He jumped down the steps, two at a time. As he rounded the second landing, he tripped, tumbled down the last flight of stairs and hit the brick floor of the basement hard.

Lux groaned as he untangled himself. "Umbra! Inquisitors are coming. You better stay down here. We don't want them to find you while you're invisible!" When he reached the chair and felt around for his sister, his stomach lurched.

6

The chair was empty.

"Umbra?" He groped around the basement, but felt no sign of his curly-haired sister. *Can this day get any worse?*

"Umbra? Where are you?"

She didn't answer, of course. Umbra didn't speak. She could laugh and cry, and once when Lux dropped a jar of fire ants in the store, she let out a loud Eek, but other than that, not a word.

The door at the top of the stairs opened and Lux paused to listen. *Maybe that's her.* He crept up the stairs, arms flung wide. "Umbra? Is that you?"

His aunt's voice answered him.

"What are you doing?" She flipped on the light. "And where is Umbra?"

Lux dropped his arms. Clearly this was going to be one of those days where everything went wrong. Lux had those days a lot. He took a deep breath, looked straight at his aunt's sensible shoes and blurted out the whole story.

"...but then when I got back down here, Umbra was gone. I thought that was her closing the door, but I guess it was you." He dropped his shoulders. "I don't know what to do."

"Well, I do." She turned and held the door open for him. "Come along," she said. "We don't have much time."

Lux hesitated. *Why do I feel like I'm going to be grounded and scrubbing the toilet in the customer bathroom for the rest of my life?*

7

"Come on," she said. "This is not the end of the world."

Lux stared. "You're kidding right? Inquisitors are coming here, probably to arrest Umbra, and maybe me since it's my fault she's invisible. That pretty much seems like the end of the world to me."

Aunt Sophia cocked her head to one side. "Do you think you're the first person to vanish their sister? Not by a long shot," she said. "Just be glad she's only invisible, and not actually missing. Finding an invisible Umbra in this store will be a lot easier than trying to locate one who could be anywhere on Earth." She leaned forward and whispered, "I speak from experience. Now, come on!"

Lux stepped through the door as his aunt hurried to the telephone behind the sales counter. Lux followed and found her talking to Leeward Spinnet.

Leeward Spinnet? Seriously? The guy is nuts!

"Wonderful, Leeward! We'll see you soon." His aunt hung up the phone.

"Aunt Sophia? Are...aren't you going to call someone else?" he asked. "Anybody?"

"No. Mr. Spinnet is on his way and should be here shortly," she answered. Seeing the look on his face, she added, "He will be able to help us. You give him far too little credit, Lux."

"No! I like him just fine. He's a lot of fun, but don't you know anyone who would be more...um..."

8

Lux searched through the words that came to mind. Competent? Intelligent? Sane? He settled on, "helpful?"

Aunt Sophia narrowed her eyes. "The only thing you need to worry about is filling your mother in on your escapades of this morning. I will worry about Mr. Spinnet, and whether or not he's helpful enough."

His mother stood across the store, staring at the front door. She was running a duster over the mummified monkey hands, which kept grabbing the feathers and pulling them out. Lux knew she'd be mad at him for turning Umbra invisible. His usual nervous hiccups gathered in his throat.

"Mom," he said, "I have to tell you something."

She kept her eyes on the door. "Hmmm?"

Lux took a breath and hiccupped. Where to start? Peas? Strawberries? Umbra's in the basement, invisible? Before he could say a word, a shadow crossed her face and he knew without looking. *Inquisitors.*

They came through the door, four of them.

Four? There's usually only three.

The Inquisitors looked like business men turned thieves in their identical grey suits. Black handkerchiefs with a red "I" embroidered on them peeked out of their breast pockets. Three of them wore snug hoods that covered their faces. A square cut-out exposed their eyes with another red "I" on the forehead. The fourth man did not wear a hood. Instead he sported a black fur hat with ear flaps tied on top. Metallic sunglasses covered his eyes and a gold medallion etched with symbols hung on the front of the hat.

What's with that hat? Inquisitors always wear hoods.

He glanced at Aunt Sophia, who was also staring at the man. *I bet it means he's an expert or something.*

Lux's eyes widened as he remembered a story his dad once told him about Inquisitors who could see things not visible.

Oh no! I bet he's an Invisi-quisitor!

Chapter Two

"You are not welcome in this store," Lux's mother said to the man in the hat. "Get out!"

"Mom!" Lux didn't claim to be an expert on Inquisitors, but making them mad seemed like a real bad idea.

"You don't give the orders here, Cerridwyn," said the man.

"Don't call me that." His mother's face went white.

Lux tried to imagine how she knew the man. His family didn't associate with Inquisitors.

"Changed your name, have you?" The man removed his sunglasses and Lux gasped. His eyes held no color, just a small black pupil in the center of a white eyeball. A scar cut across one eye and the lower lid drooped, glistening and red. It reminded Lux of the blind cave fish in his Ancient Species book.

"As a matter of fact, I have changed my name," Cerri said. "It's Mrs. St. Clare now."

"My condolences," said the man.

"Get out," his mother repeated. "Now! The other Inquisitors can do the inspection, but you, Ambrose Murklin, are not welcome."

"Too bad," said Murklin. "We're not here to inspect your inventory, *Mrs. St. Clare.* I've received information that someone on this premises is using the power of invisibility."

The blood drained from Lux's face and his heart pounded. He crossed his arms over his chest so the Inquisitors wouldn't hear it. *How do they know about Umbra?*

"No one listed as a resident here is registered with that gift," said Murklin. "Nor do I see anyone wearing a location device. Therefore, we can only assume that you have on your premises an unregistered Vanishman." He spoke just above a whisper. "I can't tell you what a pleasure it would be to arrest you for aiding and abetting a criminal."

Lux's mother glared into Murklin's blank white eyes. "That is completely ridiculous. Invisibility is not a gift that runs in our family, as you well know. And your insinuation that we're harboring an unregistered Vanishman comes awfully close to slander. I don't suppose you can tell me where you got your information?"

"Of course not," said Murklin. "You know as well as I do that our sources are confidential and protected by—"

"Yes, I know," she said. "The Information Act of 1485. A very convenient shield for the Inquisitorial Board when they can't come up with any real evidence." She threw up her hands. "Fine. Search the store, but I guarantee you won't find anything." She leaned against the shelves behind the counter. Aunt Sophia stood next to her, her hand still on the phone.

Murklin motioned to one of the Inquisitors, who stepped forward and set a black briefcase on the sales counter. Murklin opened the case and removed what looked like a pair of night-vision goggles. Lux stared as the man strapped the glasses around his head.

"These," he said as he adjusted the fit, "are heat sensing noculars."

"Fascinating," said Cerri.

Murklin gave a thin lipped smile. "Now, now, let's do try and get along. After all, you may be taking a nice long ride with us when this is all over."

Lux's stomach threatened to spill its lunch. *Is that true? Mom might be arrested?* He turned to his aunt, who looked at him and winked. Lux hiccupped.

She's lost her mind. Umbra's invisible. Murklin's got glasses that can see her and when he does, he's going to haul Mom off to jail. And Aunt Sophia's winking?

13

Then, salvation arrived. Granted, it arrived in the form of Leeward Spinnet, who today wore a long purple tunic, yellow high tops and antique motorcycle goggles. But it seemed like salvation at the time. He burst out of the storeroom, carrying a duffel bag. Ignoring the Inquisitors, he stormed up to Lux and threw the duffel at his feet.

"Leave dead squirrels on my doorstep again, young man, and I will see to it that your quibbles shrivel up and refuse to lay!" He turned to Cerri. "I say, Madam, that boy of yours needs two cents for his head and another for his pocket. Whatever will you do with him?"

"Mr. Spinnet, I am very sorry," said Aunt Sophia. "I'll make certain no more dead squirrels find their way to your door." She glared at Lux.

"Wha—" said Lux.

Turning back to Spinnet, Aunt Sophia said, "Please accept our deepest apologies."

Spinnet snapped his heels together. "Apologies? Whatever shall I do with those? Nail clippers! That's what a man needs." He turned and glanced around the store then made a beeline for the bins of rough stones.

Murklin glanced at Cerri. "You always did keep interesting company." He looked at the ceiling while fiddling with a dial on the side of the glasses. A red light began to glow in the center of each lens and a low hum filled the room.

"There we go. Now…" He turned in a circle as he surveyed the store. "These noculars eliminate virtually all visual distraction, honing in only on those items which emit heat. If our Vanishman is here, we will find him, as long as he's not dead of course." He smiled again. "What a pity that would be."

Murklin walked all around the shop. When he entered the storeroom, Lux remembered his grimoires on the basement table.

Who cares about grimiores? I'd rather pay a fine for that than have Mom or Umbra arrested.

Ten minutes later, Murklin stomped up the stairs and out of the storeroom, still wearing the glasses.

He didn't find Umbra!

"I will need to search the living quarters now," he said.

Lux's family lived on the two floors above the store. *Could Umbra have gone up there?*

"Absolutely not!" Cerri started toward Murklin. One of the Inquisitors grabbed her.

"Careful now," Murklin said. "As I said before, you're not in a position to give orders."

"That's out of the question!" his mother shouted. "I'd rather die than have you poking around--"

Murklin's smile disappeared. "That can be arranged."

"Mom!" said Lux. "Calm down."

15

"Lux is right, Cerri," said Aunt Sophia. "Mr. Murklin, we have nothing to hide. The stairway to the upper floors is in the back."

Murklin went up the stairway. The third step squeaked as he climbed. About that time, Leeward Spinnet noticed the Inquisitors.

"Dear goodness me." He stared into one of the Inquisitors eye holes. "Are these mannequins? What sort of fashion is this you've got for sale here? Well, I dare say, it's not selling is it?" He laughed. "See here? You've three identical suits and not one's sold." He shook his head and ambled back to the storeroom. As he pulled the door open, Aunt Sophia stopped him.

"Ah, Mr. Spinnet. I am afraid you've forgotten the way out again. You see, sir, it's this way." She pointed toward the front door.

Spinnet puffed out his cheeks. "Well certainly, if that's the way you're going!" He charged through the store, purple tunic flapping. "But who said I was going that way? The service in this establishment has always been ticklish." He stormed out the door.

Lux glanced at the Inquisitors. They hadn't moved. *Some salvation. All Spinnet did was prove what a freak he is and bring us some dead squirrels.*

He kicked the duffel bag at his feet, wondering if it really was filled with squirrels. Judging by his kick, it was filled with something harder than dead rodents, but then, maybe squirrels got hard when they died. Who knew? It didn't really matter now that everyone he loved was going to be hauled away to prison.

"Did I tell you," his aunt said, "about the time—"

She stopped as Murklin clomped down the stairs.

"Well?" Cerri asked.

Murklin tore off the goggles and threw them into the case. "Not the cleanest of homes, I must say, but nothing invisible, today. However, I am going to put you on probation."

"Probation?" said Cerri. "You can't be serious! We haven't done anything wrong."

"I am serious, Mrs. St. Clare." His eerie eyes never blinked. "And if I were you, I'd watch my step very carefully in the weeks to come. I'm not convinced of your innocence. I'll be visiting again, soon." He snapped the nocular case shut and swung it off the counter. "Oh, and if you happen to see Atlas, give him my best." He turned and walked out, followed by the Inquisitors.

"Probation!" said his mom. "Do you realize what that's going to do to our sales?" Her eyes filled with tears. "That man is evil itself. To think he and Atlas used to be friends. 'If I see Atlas'." She turned to Aunt Sophia and whispered, "Do you think he knows something?"

"Knows something?" Lux asked. "About what?"

"Never you mind," said his aunt.

"Something about Dad?" Lux frowned. "You said he was on a business trip."

"He is," his mother said.

"Then what--"

"You heard your mother," said Aunt Sophia. *Something's not right.* "Is Dad still coming home on Monday?" Lux asked.

"Lux," Aunt Sophia said. "Isn't there something you need to tell your mother?"

Cerri glanced from Aunt Sophia to Lux and raised her eyebrows. "What's going on here that I don't know about?"

Lux explained about his pea tonic. "And now, I don't know where Umbra is. Aunt Sophia called Spinnet and then..."

His aunt patted his shoulder. "Everything is fine. You'll find Umbra in the basement where Leeward sent her. In fact, I imagine he's made it back by now as well. Shall we all go down?"

They followed her to the basement and found Leeward Spinnet sitting on an upturned bucket. He read out loud from the back of an incense box and he held his arms at odd angles, as if something sat on his lap.

"Umbra!" shouted Lux.

Spinnet fell to the ground as Umbra leapt up. "Great gherkins!" he cried.

Cerri hugged and patted her invisible daughter.

18

"How did you find her?" Lux asked. "And how come Murklin didn't see her?"

"Ah, yes," said the old man. "The predictable foibles of those fashion faux-pasers." He stroked his short beard. "Machines fail, Lux. Yes, they do."

Lux sighed and turned to his aunt. "What the heck is he talking about?"

"I think what Mr. Spinnet means—" said Aunt Sophia.

"By all means, call me Chancellor," Spinnet interrupted.

"— is that the Inquisitors depend heavily on machines to discover and decode magic. They have a great disdain for magic, even when it's used for good reasons. The problem with machines, though, is that sometimes they fail, sometimes they break and, most importantly, they can be fooled which is what happened today.

"When Mr. Murklin strapped on his goggles, he told us they could detect heat and nothing more. All Leeward had to do was pick Umbra up and hold her close to him. His heat and her heat were indiscernible to those special glasses. To Mr. Murklin, it just looked as though Leeward was sifting through the stone bins. When Murklin went upstairs, Leeward walked Umbra to the back of the store. When I directed Leeward to use the front door, it created enough of a distraction that Umbra was able to slip through the storeroom door unnoticed and creep down here. One of your better plans, if I do say so, Leeward."

Lux stared at the old man. *I can't believe he came up with a plan that actually worked.*

Spinnet tried to bite a button off his tunic.

"But how did he know where Umbra was?" Lux asked.

"Umbra who?" said the old man.

"Among his many other talents, Leeward has the unique ability to see invisible beings," said his aunt. "In his earlier days, when the government was more magic-friendly, Leeward served as an investigator for them."

Lux gasped. "An Invisi-quistor?"

"No, no!" she said. "Invisi-quisitor's were used to hunt down witches with vanishing abilities. Mr. Spinnet has never served the Corps in that capacity. But he was one of the best investigators they've ever had."

So, Spinnet's not such a nutcase after all. Even with all the wild outfits, crazy sayings and…

"Hey! Wait a minute," he said. "What about those dead squirrels?"

Spinnet leapt onto the table. "Where? Keep them away! Oh, dark days indeed!"

Aunt Sophia frowned at Lux. "I expect you'll find that duffel is full of certain out-of-print herbal encyclopedias and grimoires. Not to mention, several vials of poisonous spiders and a jar of vampire bat blood. None of which you're supposed to have," she

20

said. "You must be more careful, Lux. I'm surprised you didn't think about those with Murklin poking around down here."

"I didn't know the Inquisitors were coming," said Lux. "Besides, Murklin couldn't see the books. They don't emit heat so they wouldn't have shown up in his goggles, right?"

"Lux, dear," said his aunt. "Do you really think three Inquisitors and a Corps official came here today, unannounced, because they heard someone in our store might be invisible?"

"What?" Lux asked. "Why else would they…"

"Think it through."

"But Umbra was invisible…I mean she is. They must have known that!"

"Coincidence," she said. "How many reports of illegal magical activity does the Corps get each day? Thousands. Tens of thousands. Could they really spare four men to investigate each one?"

"But invisibility is a class three skill," Lux said. "They'd have to investigate that."

His aunt shook her head. "How could anyone report someone being invisible? People like Leeward are very rare these days, so there aren't many people reporting invisibility. Rarer still are Vanishmen themselves. That gift has been bred out of us, for the most part, like so many magical skills. An Inquisitor today could hunt all his life for a Vanishman and never find one. It doesn't make much sense for the

Corps to assign four men to such an unlikely task. Does it?"

"Why else would they come?" Lux asked. "What were they doing here, if it wasn't because of Umbra?"

Aunt Sophia rubbed her temples. "Another day, Lux."

"Thursday?" said Spinnet.

"Thursday it is!" agreed Aunt Sophia.

Lux threw his head back and groaned. *Nobody tells me anything.* He remembered what his mother said about Murklin--that he knew something about Atlas.

What's there to know? Mom said Dad was on a business trip. Is that not true? Did those Inquisitors have something to do with Dad?

Cerri helped Leeward down from the table. "Well," she said. "There's just one thing left to do."

Lux sighed then turned to face his mom and receive his punishment.

"What shall we try first?"

His eyes went wide. *Try first? What does that mean? How many punishments am I going to have?*

"Redunderate spell?" Aunt Sophia suggested. "We should try to undo what's been done before we try to do anything new."

"Something new, something blew, something burrowed and something..... something else..." Spinnet covered his nose with an empty mortar.

They're talking about fixing Umbra, not punishing me. At least, not yet. "I have my hellebore recipe," he said. "We can try that."

"Let's start with the simple solutions first," said his mother. "I seriously doubt we'll have to resort to potions. Your magic can't have been strong enough to cause any lasting damage. Besides, don't you have some repair work to do in the front window?"

"Oh, right," said Lux. "The scrying mirrors."

Aunt Sophia went up to the store with Lux. Cerri and Spinnet began working to restore Umbra. By the afternoon, they ran out of 'undoing' spells and started on the restorative spells.

"If these don't work," said Cerri, "we'll move on to spells and hexbreaking."

Worry niggled in Lux's stomach. *Mom's surprised they haven't fixed Umbra yet, I can tell. But I'm not the first person to vanish my sister and if anybody can help Umbra, it's mom and Aunt Sophia. I bet she'll be back to normal by dinner.*

Chapter Three

Monday morning, Lux climbed onto the school bus with his mother's warning ringing in his ears.

"Do not tell anyone, anyone what happened to Umbra," she said. "If somebody asks--"

"She's sick. I got it." Lux rolled his eyes. *Does she think I'm a moron?* Despite two whole days of spell work, his sister remained invisible.

"I'm sure it will be fine," his mom said. "Your tonic couldn't have been very strong."

"Right," he said. *And anyway, Dad will be home tonight. He'll know what to do.*

Lux settled into a seat at the back of the bus, across from his friend Jason Peppertree. "Hey Pep."

Jason gave Lux an uncharacteristic frown. "Dude? What happened this weekend?"

Lux's heart raced. "What do you mean?"

"You were supposed to meet me at the skate park yesterday," said Jason. "I waited for like ever. Where were you?"

24

Lux sighed with relief. "Oh, right. I forgot all about it."

"You forgot?" said Jason. "That's not cool."

"I'm sorry," said Lux. "I just..." He wanted Jason to know he hadn't just forgotten about him. "I...I'm sorry."

Jason shrugged. "Whatever."

"How about if we go this afternoon?" said Lux. His best friend Cyril was making his way down the aisle toward them. "You, me and Cy."

Cyril had dishwater blond hair and big red glasses and loved botany. He and Lux became best friends their first day of kindergarten, when a vial of stink dust fell out of Lux's pencil box and Cyril countered it with a soap-gas tonic.

Cyril tossed his backpack onto the seat next to Lux. "Do what this afternoon?"

"Go to the skate park," said Lux.

"Skateboarding again?" Cyril pushed his glasses further up onto his nose. "I was hoping we could go to Jason's and play Super Death Boy 5. I just got it."

Jason perked up. "You got it? No way! I thought it sold out before the stores opened."

Cyril grinned. "My mom and I camped out at Techno-Mania-Mart Friday night. We got the last one."

Jason smiled. "Sweet. But we can't go to my house. My mom's reworking the security spells on the doors. Let's go to Lux's."

25

"Okay," said Cyril.

"Oh...actually," said Lux. "We can't."

"Why?"

"Because, um..." He paused. "Because Umbra's sick."

"So?" said Jason. "We won't bother her."

"Yeah, but she's really contagious."

Cyril edged away from Lux. "With what?"

Lying made Lux nervous. "With...hic...hiccups."

Cyril raised his eyebrows. "Contagious hiccups?"

Jason shook his head. "Dude, that's pathetic. If you don't want us to come over, just say so." He picked up his books and moved to a seat further up.

Cyril watched Jason go. "What's that all about?"

"I forgot to meet him at the skate park yesterday," said Lux. "I said I was sorry. He's just mad."

"Is there something really wrong with Umbra?" Cyril asked.

Lux shrugged. "It's nothing. Mom just doesn't want people around when Umbra's not feeling good.

"Ok," said Cyril. "You can come to my house if you want. My dad made oatmeal cookies."

Lux smiled. "Cool. I'll call my mom after school and let her know." *We need to fix Umbra soon. Keeping her a secret is harder than I thought.*

The day stretched on forever. Lux hadn't done any of his homework. He scribbled answers on the way to each class so he had something to turn in.

When the final bell rang, he shuffled to the pay phone to call his mom. *Just my luck. The one day I didn't read anything, every single teacher gives a pop quiz. At least I aced the science one. Good thing we were studying ancient herbs.*

Lux dialed the store number, but his mom didn't answer. A different, familiar voice came out of the ear piece.

"Hello, caller. This is the black telephone at the back of the store. As I cannot see you, you should tell me who you are and what you want."

Lux rolled his eyes. "Mr. Spinnet?"

"Liar!" cried the old man. "You are not Mr. Spinnet, because I, in fact, am Mr. Spinnet. Strike one."

"No, I meant, you're Mr. Spinnet," said Lux.

"I've already told you that. You do not get credit for that answer."

Lux sighed and closed his eyes as he carefully chose his words. "Please may I speak with Cerri St. Clare."

"Why of course," he said. "Just one moment. Do you mind if I put you on hold?"

"S...sure." Lux bit his lip. *We don't have a hold button. What's he talking about?* A click and then a dial tone gave him the answer. Lux groaned, dug more money out of his pocket and dialed again. His mother answered.

"Mom, why is Spinnet answering the phone?"

"He's helping out in the store, just for today, while we work on…you know. Are you at school?"

"Yeah. Can I go over to Cyril's for a while?"

Cerri hesitated. "I suppose. You'll be home for dinner?"

"Definitely," he said. "I want to be there when Dad gets home."

"Oh," said Cerri. "Actually, I'm not sure he's going to make it home tonight. His business is taking a bit longer than he expected."

Lux's heart skipped a beat. "What? When is he coming home?"

"Soon. Very soon."

"Soon like, tomorrow? Or soon like, next week."

"I'm not sure. It depends on how his trip goes."

"Well, where is he? Is he okay?"

"Sweetheart, don't worry so much. I'm sure he's fine."

Lux stopped short. "You're sure he's fine? Don't you know? Haven't you talked to him?" No response. "Mom? Mom?"

"I'm here," she said. "Maybe you should just come home, Lux. I'd feel better if you were here."

"Something's wrong, isn't it?" he said. "Tell me what's going on."

His mother sighed. "Come on home. We'll talk when you get here."

Lux hung up the phone and raced to the bus circle. He wished he could teleport but, being a St. Clare, that would never be one of his gifts. He climbed onto the bus. Cyril had saved his usual seat at the back.

"Did you call your mom?" said Cyril.

"What?" said Lux.

"To see if you could come over?"

"Oh. Yeah, but Mom said I had to come straight home."

"Why?" Cyril asked.

"It's just..." Lux's mind reeled. "Family stuff."

"Is it Umbra?" Cyril whispered.

"Yeah. Do you mind if we don't talk about it right now?" The bus pulled away from the curb and rumbled up the road.

"Sure, okay," said Cyril. "But if you want to talk later..."

"Yeah, thanks."

They rode in silence. Cyril kept glancing at Lux, who gripped the seat ahead with white knuckles. When the bus stopped outside the store, Lux jumped off and ran in.

His mother came out of the storeroom with a stack of books. Leeward Spinnet stood behind the counter, having a pencil dual with a dried monkey hand.

"Where's Dad?" Lux demanded.

Cerri put the books down on a table.

Leeward glanced up and the monkey hand got in a sharp blow to his knuckles. "Ouch!" He rubbed his hand and glared at Lux. "Why are you asking me? Do I look like an Inquisitor?"

"Leeward!" cried Cerri. "We haven't...we weren't..."

Lux's stomach pitched. "Inquisitors? What do Inquisitors have to do with Dad?"

"Nothing, of course," Cerri said.

"Nothing except that they have kidnapped him," said Spinnet. "Other than that, though, she is correct. Nothing whatsoever."

Cerri put her face in her hands. "Leeward! For Brighid's sake."

"Kidnapped?" shouted Lux.

"No," Cerri said. "We have no reason to think he's been kidnapped."

"Where is he then?"

"We don't know," she said.

"Oh, well that's reassuring," cried Lux.

"He was working on a project with your Uncle Crowley and they lost contact last week."

"You mean Crowley's missing too?" Hot tears stung his eyes.

"No. Well, yes," said his mother. "I mean, we're not sure."

"You're really not good at this reassuring thing, Mom."

His mother walked over and put her arms around him. "I'm sorry, Lux. I hadn't intended to tell you this way." She cast an angry glance toward Leeward, who resumed his pencil fight. "I hadn't intended to tell you at all that we suspected…"

"So you do think Dad has been kidnapped." Lux shrugged off his mothers arms and looked at the old man. "Well, I'm glad Spinnet told me. I'd rather know the truth than not know anything. Where were they? How did it happen?"

"They were working on a project. They got separated and your father didn't…" Tears pooled in his mother's eyes. "Your uncle waited for hours, but Atlas never showed up. Crowley called to tell us what happened then went out looking."

"Where is Crowley now?"

His mother shrugged. "We last heard from him three days ago. He said he had one more place to check."

"And where was that?"

"He…didn't say."

I can't believe this! Dad? Kidnapped by Inquisitors? That stuff doesn't happen anymore. Does it?

"What are we going to do?" Lux asked.

"Rise up and fight, you mindless coward," Spinnet shouted at the monkey hand.

"We wait," said his mother. "We wait and we hope." She hugged him again.

"I think I like Spinnet's suggestion a lot better."

31

Chapter Four

For the rest of the week, Lux woke to the sound of Aunt Sophia's hard shoes clomping up the stairs. She arrived early each morning to help Cerri work on Umbra. Things weren't going well. The hex-breaking tea of huckleberry and chili powder gave her a tummy ache. Umbra's skin itched from the revealing salve and the cedar smudging made her sneeze. Lux felt more guilty every day.

Aunt Sophia wrote a letter to the school principal explaining Umbra had chicken pox. To keep Lux from getting it, she claimed they were keeping Umbra under quarantine at Six Mile Farm.

But everyone, probably even Leeward Spinnet, knew chicken pox only lasted a week. If they didn't fix Umbra soon, the Inquisitors would come back. And if that happened... Lux tried not to think of the consequences.

The phone rang, startling Lux out of his bleak thoughts. "I got it. Hello?"

"Lux!" said his friend, Otis Huston. "My mom is freaking out. She says she can't pick you, me, Umbra and Carrie up Friday after the show. Can one of your parents do it?"

Lux dropped his head into his hand. "The Cirque de Magique! I totally forgot it's this weekend. Otis, I'm sorry. I don't think we can go."

"What? You have to go," said Otis. "We already got the tickets."

"Yeah, but Umbra's still sick."

"So? Carrie can find another friend to go with her ticket. The question is, can your mom pick us up?"

"I don't think so. Maybe you could find somebody else for my ticket too."

"Lux." Otis sounded irritated. "What is up with you lately? You keep flaking out on everybody."

"Look, I'm sorry. I can't go, okay? My dad's out of town and my mom can't leave Umbra to pick us up. I just...I can't go."

"Fine," snapped Otis.

"I'm sorry," said Lux. He heard a click and realized Otis hung up.

Great. Jason's still not speaking to me. I had to cancel the sleepover with Marx and now Otis is mad too. If Umbra doesn't get fixed soon, I won't have any friends left.

Lux pulled his hair into a rubber band, put on a T-shirt and headed downstairs for breakfast. The living room, kitchen and dining room occupied the second floor, above the store. A small laundry room stood behind the kitchen. Lux's father's study filled the round turret above the store's display window and a large balcony off the dining room looked down onto Fort Street. The store had always been home to Lux and Umbra, and their mom too. In fact, Pickingills had occupied the store since the day it opened, over one hundred and eighty years ago.

Lux heard his mom talking to Umbra in the kitchen as he reached the foot of the stairs. They planned to try some sort of paste remedy today. Cerri was trying to corral her daughter's curls into a plastic shower cap--a tough job even when she could see Umbra's hair. With her unruly curls invisible, the task proved impossible.

"It's like pushing honey uphill!" Cerri threw down the shower cap. "I give up. Let her hair turn green—maybe we'll be able to see it that way."

Aunt Sophia reread the instructions from the spell book and gave the potion three deliberate stirs. "That should do it for now. It will be ready in thirteen minutes. Just enough time to get breakfast for you, young man! What will it be? Creamy wheat or toaster-what-nots?"

Neither sounded very appealing with the green goo bubbling in the cauldron behind her. "I'm not very hungry."

Lux recognized the smell. *A Restorative Paste? Gimme a break!* Lux made that potion all the time. It worked great on the scrapes he got while skateboarding, but he knew it would not *restore* Umbra to sight.

"Any word from Dad?" Lux asked.

"No." His mom tried to hide a sniffle. "But I'm sure we'll hear something today."

She said that yesterday too.

He looked across the table. Umbra had chosen the toaster-what-nots. Lux could tell because little toast crusts lined up along the patterns in the table cloth. His sister never ate the crust of anything. Lux was staring at the crumbs, contemplating his father's whereabouts, when something dawned on him.

"Mom—what happens to the food invisible people eat? Does it become invisible when they swallow it?"

"It depends on what is making the person invisible. If it's a charm, then most anything they touch would become invisible. If it's a spell, only the things they were touching when the spell hit them would be invisible. And for Vanishmen, their skill would only affect their body—not the clothes they were wearing or anything they were touching. For example, when a Vanishman eats food, it remains visible for quite a while, until it's absorbed by the body."

"Well, then..." Lux paused, wondering why his mom and aunt didn't pick up on it. "Doesn't that

35

mean Umbra's invisibility is caused by a charm? I can't see the toaster pop-up she just ate and her clothes are invisible. Unless she's still wearing the same ones she was wearing when it happened, her clothes wouldn't be invisible if it's a spell. Right?"

Cerri turned to look at Umbra, her mouth open.

"Great Scott! The boy's right. I should have seen it," said Aunt Sophia. "Leeward even pointed it out the other night! 'A new dress again, cherub?' He couldn't have been clearer." She turned to Cerri. "Well, this gives us a plan of attack, doesn't it? What shall we try first?"

Lux left them to it, as he saw the school bus coming down Fort Street. He rushed to gather up his books and managed to catch the bus as it came back up the next block. The day proved to be a long one, with none of his homework done and Cyril out sick. Otis and Jason wouldn't speak to him, so Lux ate lunch with the magic nerds. His thoughts switched from whether his mom could remove the charm causing Umbra's invisibility to where his dad might be.

By the time Lux got home, he just knew he would walk in and find Umbra restored to sight. He raced off the bus, stormed into the store and crashed straight into Leeward Spinnet.

"Galloping galoshes, Boy! Did that bus drop you off or shoot you in?" The old man gathered

36

himself up and cinched his satin smoking jacket tight over his striped running tights.

"Sorry Mr. Spinnet," said Lux. He unhooked the buckle of his backpack from Spinnet's feathered hat. "I didn't see you there."

"Didn't see me where?" The old man glanced around. "Are you sure it wasn't me? What didn't I look like?"

Lux stared at him, unsure how to respond. "Uh...you didn't look like yourself."

"Well, that's probably why!" Spinnet took the hat Lux passed him. "Thank you, son. Now, get along, little doggie. Yippee ki yay!"

Lux ran upstairs, burst through the back door and dropped his backpack in the middle of the laundry room floor. Silence enveloped the house. He slowed to a tiptoe as he entered the kitchen.

Whoa!

Every cabinet, every drawer stood open, their contents strewn onto the countertop and the floor. Piles of dried herbs laid everywhere. Books covered the stove. Yellowed parchments hung on the refrigerator with magnets. Flowers, dried animal parts, bits of fabric and thread littered the room. Lux spun around with his mouth open.

What happened in here? Did somebody get attacked? "Mom?"

A tired voice answered from the living room. "In here, Lux."

He crept through the mess, trying not to step on anything too valuable, and found his mother and aunt stretched out on chairs in the living room. Neither of them moved when he walked in.

"Where's Umbra?" he asked. His mother gestured to the couch, where the last cushion looked dented. "I saw Mr. Spinnet downstairs. What's he doing here?"

"Leeward was kind enough to take over the store for us so we could spend the day working with Umbra," said his aunt.

Ouch. I bet the store is more of a mess than the kitchen, and all for nothing. Umbra's still invisible. Lux sighed.

His mother sat up. "How was school today? How is Cyril? I haven't seen him since...well..." She glanced at Umbra. "I'm sorry, Lux. This must be very hard on you and all of our attention has been on Umbra."

"No!" Lux protested. "It's fine. I want you to pay attention to Umbra. After all, it's my fault she's like this."

His mother and aunt exchanged glances. "Actually, Lux," said his mom. "There's no way this could be your fault."

"What?" he asked.

"This is a really strong charm," she said. "Some kind of old magic, we think. It's not something you could have accidentally done to Umbra. It would take days of concentrated workings, at the right astrological time, to produce a charm like this. There's really no way this was any of your doing."

"It wasn't my pea tonic?" he said.

"No. I'm afraid not," said his mom.

Lux thought he should feel relieved, but he didn't. "It sounds like you know what charm it is."

"Yes...and no," said his aunt. "We don't know what it is, but we do know what it isn't. And what it isn't, isn't good."

"You sound like Spinnet," Lux said. "What does that mean?"

His aunt rubbed her head. "There are many types of charms, Lux, but they generally fall into two categories. The first type of charm works using lesser magic and they're very simple things. If you want to ensure good harvest, you carry kernels of corn in your right pocket. If you want money, you wear green and gold clothing. These charms get gradually more complicated, but they all follow the same simple premise: if you want something, carry something that represents it.

"The second type uses greater or 'ritual' magic and there is nothing simple about ritual magic. This is the type of magic the Inquisitors most fear and with good reason. Of all the branches of magic, ritual magic is the most powerful and the one most often used on the left hand path."

"What's that?" Lux said. "The left hand path?"

"It means using magic to evil ends," said Aunt Sophia. "Nearly every evil magical deed ever performed, in the history of the world, was done through ritual magic. It traces its roots to the ancient texts and some parts of ritual magic are older even than the written word. The power of ritual is limitless."

Lux thought he might drown in words. Questions filled his mind but he didn't know which to ask first. "Okay, so... How is that making Umbra invisible? Why would anybody want to do that? And if ritual magic is so evil, why don't the Inquisitors outlaw it?"

"Just a minute. No one said ritual magic was evil," his aunt said. "Far from it. The vast majority of ritual magic is used for good—powerful good. It is unfortunate, however, that this same power can be corrupted by those with the desire to work harm. The sad fact is, ritual magic has been outlawed. It's one of the worst things the government has ever done." She scowled and even his mother shook her head.

"If bad people use it so much, why do you care if it's outlawed?" said Lux.

"You're too young to understand," his mother replied.

"Soon, Lux. Soon you'll be old enough," said his aunt.

"Soon!" he cried. "I'm sick of soon. Soon I'll use real poisons. Soon I'll understand. Soon Dad will be home. But soon never comes, does it?" Anger welled up inside Lux, and a week's worth of pent-up emotion spilled out. "Can you at least tell me what any of that 'greater' and 'lesser' stuff has to do with Umbra? And why you can't fix her? Because it sounds like you're giving up." Close to tears, Lux decided to stop talking. He walked over to the balcony doors and stared at nothing.

"Lux," his mother said. "I'm sorry it seems like you're in the dark on so much of what's going on. I really wish it could be different, but you'll just have to trust me. You're not ready for this stuff yet. When you are, I will explain it. I promise."

"Whatever." *I'm sick of adults treating me like a baby.* "What about Umbra's charm," he asked. "Is there anything you can tell me about that?"

"Yes," said his aunt. "We have determined what the charm is not, as I have said. It is not a lesser magic charm. Lesser magic charms must remain in contact with the body to work. We took off everything Umbra had on, all her jewelry and hair baubles and such. She had several cleansing baths, to remove any oils or perfumes, as well as smoke smudgings and fannings. But after a day of extensive Umbra-cleaning, she is still invisible."

"So, it's a greater magic charm," Lux said. "How do we get rid of those? Are there books? Let's make a list. Let's get working on it." No one moved. They just sat in their chairs and stared at the floor. "Why aren't we getting to work? What aren't you telling me?"

"Actually, it's something we've already told you," his mom said. "Ritual magic is illegal.

41

Removing a ritual magic charm requires the use of ritual magic. There's nothing we can do."

Deflated, Lux sank into a chair. "No cure? What about school? If she doesn't go soon, the Inquisitors will find out she's invisible."

His mother nodded.

This can't be happening. Dad would know what to do, but where is he? Lux couldn't sit still. He went back to the balcony door and stared across the street. His mind churned with worry.

We can't wait for Dad. We have to do something now, before Umbra goes to prison. He replayed his aunt's words. 'Removing a ritual magic charm requires the use of ritual magic.'

"So, it's not impossible to cure Umbra, just illegal?" he asked.

"Illegal, impossible," said his aunt. "It amounts to the same thing. Ritual magic is the only offense that carries the death penalty, and an invisible Umbra is better than…well, losing anyone we love."

Death penalty? "But aren't we already breaking the law by hiding Umbra's invisibility? If we cure Umbra from being illegal…is that still illegal?"

"Lux," said his aunt. "Put it out of your mind. It is not worth the risk."

But if the Inquisitors didn't detect it… I bet I could do it. I'm sure I could. I just need to find the right spell. Lux's mind raced with the possibility. *If I cure Umbra, my life goes back to normal. I'll have friends again and Umbra can go back to school. If I can find the right spell…*

And if the Inquisitors don't find out. And if I can do it right, with no accidents... If...

For a word with only two letters, 'if' seemed pretty overwhelming.

For several minutes, no one said a word. A couple black crows cawed outside and one settled on the balcony rail, pecking at the flowers in the window box. Lux sat lost in his thoughts for what seemed like hours. But then the sound of heavy footsteps thundered up the back stairs.

Chapter Five

Lux leapt from his chair and rushed to stand with his mother and aunt. The footsteps thudded to the top of the stairs. The back door banged open. Lux glanced around for a weapon, but all he found was the broom from the fireplace set. He grabbed it and held it up.

"Cerri?" called a familiar voice. "Whoa! What happened in--"

"Is that..." said Cerri.

Lux dropped the broom. "Crowley!"

They rushed into the kitchen, all talking to Crowley at the same time. By the time they made their way back into the living room, Lux's uncle had been brought up to date on everything that had happened since he left. He was amazed at Umbra's invisibility, but more shocked that Cerri left Leeward Spinnet in control of the store for a whole day.

"Really, Cer. The guy is nuts!" he said.

Aunt Sophia frowned. "Crowley! A little respect, please!"

"I know, AnSo," as Crowley called his aunt. "Spinnet was the be-all, end-all way back when, and he's a super guy. Really! But it's not all clicking for him anymore." Crowley sank onto the sofa and put his feet up on the coffee table. "D'you know what he said when I walked in? He asked me what he would look like if I hadn't seen him. What does that mean?"

Everyone laughed, except of course Aunt Sophia.

Crowley laid his head back on the couch. "I am so glad to see you guys."

Lux sat down next to Crowley, propping his dirty sneakers next to his uncle's worn black boots. He felt the couch shift a bit as Umbra crawled onto Crowley's lap.

"Any luck?" his mother asked.

Crowley's hand bounced in mid-air as he patted Umbra on the head. "Some."

"What?" asked Lux. "You saw Dad?"

"No, but I managed to get into Sprenger's tunnels," said Crowley.

"Into what?" said Lux.

"The good news is that he's not there," Crowley said. "At least, not anymore."

"But he *was* there?" Cerri asked. Lines of worry creased her forehead.

"Yeah. But apparently he found some way to escape. That nearly pushed Sprenger over the edge.

45

He ranted and raved for days. I've never seen him so angry!"

"Dad was in a *cell*?" asked Lux. "Why?"

"I don't know how Atlas escaped," Crowley said. "They were keeping him in one of the lower tunnel cells and nobody's ever escaped from those before. Sprenger figured Atlas had help from one of the guards, so he had them all thrown into cells themselves. That's when I left. I figured if Atlas wasn't there then there wasn't much point in me sticking around."

Lux grabbed his uncle's arm. "What tunnels are you talking about? Was Dad arrested?"

"Do you know who Sprenger is?" Crowley asked.

Lux said, "You mean Jules Sprenger?"

At the same time, his mother said, "Crowley, I really don't think Lux needs to know...."

Crowley looked at Cerri, and then at Lux. "Sorry, Lux. It's up to your mom."

"Mom!" Lux yelled.

"I'm sorry, Lux," she said. "I know you're tired of hearing it, but you're just too young."

He opened his mouth to protest, but to his surprise, his aunt beat him to it.

"Cerri," she said, "I think in this case it would be best if Lux knew the whole story."

Lux nodded. "She's right, Mom."

Cerri sighed. "Well, ok." Umbra, much younger than Lux, lucked out by being invisible, and Cerri neglected to send her out of the room.

"You know Jules Sprenger," said Crowley. "Head of the Conventional Defense League, the branch of the government that runs the prisons. What most people don't know is that underneath National Prison is a whole network of tunnels. Sprenger uses them for the headquarters of a very secret group, an army actually, called the MM. No one outside the order knows what MM stands for, but we call them Murklin's Murderers."

"Murklin?" Lux asked.

"Ambrose Murklin. He's Sprenger's right-arm man, heads up the army."

"But he was here!" Lux shouted.

"Murklin was here?" Crowley asked. "In the store?"

Lux nodded.

"It was a surprise inspection," said Cerri. "He and three inquisitors showed up claiming they'd had a report of a Vanishman on the premises. They searched the whole place, and of course, found nothing."

"Right. Because they were actually looking for Atlas...or me." Crowley whistled through his teeth. "Wow. I can't believe he sent Murklin. Sprenger's getting desperate to try a stunt like that. Inquisitors are not allowed to show up unannounced. Why didn't you report them?"

"Umbra was invisible and Atlas was missing. The last thing I wanted was more people crawling around here," said Cerri.

"Right." Crowley wrinkled his brow. "Now I'm worried. I thought you guys would be safe, but if Inquisitor's are coming around unannounced, who knows what they'll do next. I don't want the MM showing up here."

"The murderers?" Lux gasped.

"Crowley!" said his mother. "You were going to explain the tunnels; that's all."

"Sorry," said Crowley. "So, back to the tunnels. Underneath National Prison are these tunnels. They used to be canals, long time ago, when they floated cargo into Capital City from the farming towns. At the turn of the century, they drained the water and covered them with big steel plates to make roads. Everybody forgot the canals were there. Nine or ten years ago, Sprenger caught a prisoner trying to escape through one; that prisoner was Ambrose Murklin. In exchange for not killing him, Sprenger made Murklin draw up maps of the canal system. Since then, Sprenger's added a whole bunch of additional tunnels, rooms and cells; all completely unknown, officially anyway, by the government."

"So, Dad was in one of those cells?" said Lux.

"For a while," Crowley replied. "But then he broke out. I've been looking for him, but I just....." He shrugged. "I just don't know where else to look."

"Crowley, you've done so much already," Cerri said. "Atlas knew the risk he was taking when he left. We both did. But the need was too great. You two did what you set out to do and the magical world is better for it."

"What did you guys do?" Lux asked.

Cerri smiled at her brother. "We'll find Atlas. I know we will. He's alive and he's free. It's just a matter of time before he makes his way home."

"But what did you guys do that we're better for?" Lux asked. No one even spared him a glance.

"Yeah, about that being free part..." said Crowley. "Sprenger knows I've been poking around, so my apartment's probably not the safest place to be. I was hoping I could hang here with you, but I don't want to bring you any more trouble. Maybe I should head back out."

"Certainly not," Aunt Sophia said. "You will be perfectly safe in the basement. I think it's best for you to stay close to home."

"They'll be sending more Inquisitors," Crowley warned.

"They already sent their best," Cerri pointed out. "We got through that fine. I'll feel better knowing you're here, Crowley."

"All righty then," he grinned. "I was hoping you'd say that! To the basement it is."

"The basement?" Lux wrinkled his nose. "Hello? They searched the basement last time. Crowley can't hide there."

49

"Not that basement," his uncle laughed. "I'll be in the...what? The second basement?"

"Yes," said Aunt Sophia.

Lux's mouth fell open. "We have two basements?"

"I'll get some blankets and things for you," said Cerri, walking toward the stairs.

"Wait. We have more than one basement?" Lux repeated.

"I left my duffel bag in the hall," Crowley said. "I'll take it down a little later. When should we go, AnSo?"

"Perhaps it would be best to wait until dusk. With the rush hour, and the changing of day to night, there should be enough shifting energy to hide the bit of flux we'll make."

"Great. Time for a snooze." Crowley settled back onto the couch, with his arms behind his head.

"Hey!" Lux shouted. Everyone turned to look at him. "Since when do we have two basements?"

"You don't have two basements, Lux," replied his uncle.

Lux's eyebrows drew together. "We...we don't have two basements?"

"No. There's...I don't know, three or four—"

"Crowley!" warned Aunt Sophia. "That's enough."

"Oh...sorry. Maybe you guys should make a list of things I'm not supposed to tell the kids," he said.

50

"We have four basements?" Lux didn't expect an answer.

Cerri climbed the stairs to get Crowley's blankets. Aunt Sophia went into the kitchen and began cleaning. Crowley leaned back and closed his eyes again. Umbra seemed to be sleeping at the far end of the couch. Lux walked over and patted around until he found her head. To his surprise, she took his hand.

"Umbra, did you know we had more than one basement?" he asked.

She squeezed his hand once. Once for yes, twice for no. That was the code.

"You did?" How much else did Umbra know? "Did you know about Murklin and tunnels and all that other stuff?" Two squeezes. "What about Dad? Do you know why they're chasing him?" Two soft squeezes. *Well, at least I'm not the last to know about everything.*

The three of them sat on the couch. Crowley and Umbra dozed as Lux mulled over everything that just happened. The room grew darker as the sun shifted through the sky. When Aunt Sophia came in from straightening the kitchen, shadows filled the living room.

"Crowley," she whispered.

He roused. "Is it time?"

"Yes, I think so," she said. "Leave the lights off. We'll retrieve your luggage on the way. Cerri

51

has already gone down with the blankets." She turned to Lux. "Where is Umbra?"

"She's asleep, there." He pointed to the pillows on the arm of the couch.

"Fine," she said. "You'll come with us."

"Really?" Lux grinned. He could find out for himself about these other basements.

"Yes, but be quiet." She wagged her finger under Lux's nose. "It is imperative that we have as little noise as possible. Understood?"

He nodded. Aunt Sophia turned and walked through the kitchen door, followed by Crowley and Lux. Once they reached the stairs, Crowley picked up his canvas bag and eased it over his shoulder. Aunt Sophia gave Lux one last 'shhh' before they started down the stairs. At the bottom, she peered around the door jamb into the store.

"All clear," she murmured.

They crossed the store room and made their way down the basement stairs. Lux stopped at the bottom and looked for the stairs to the next basement. Aunt Sophia and Crowley went straight to his worktable, still strewn with the herbs from his peas-to-strawberries potion.

Wow. I haven't done any potions work in almost a week! That's gotta be the longest I've ever gone without cooking up something.

Aunt Sophia crossed to the blank wall opposite the table. A rickety chair leaned against the wall with a stack of blankets on it. His aunt picked up the blankets and motioned for Lux to take the small cooler sitting on the floor.

"Back up a bit, please," she said. As they did, Aunt Sophia put out her right hand. She held her palm to the wall at eye level.

At first nothing happened. Lux wondered if they were just teasing him about the other basements.

But then, the stone around his aunt's hand began to glow. A reddish light crept across the face of the wall, making a large circle. The light grew so bright Lux couldn't look at it.

His aunt started chanting. Lux put his arm up to block some of the light coming out of the wall. As he did, the strangest sensation came over him. A wave of warmth rippled through his body. He reached out to steady himself against the table and found it wasn't there. The basement was empty. Where his aunt held her hand stood an open archway leading to a set of stone steps. Lux's jaw dropped.

"Wow," said Crowley. "That still gives me goose bumps."

"That went well," Aunt Sophia said. "We'll ask Cerri if she noticed any energy backlash." She turned to Crowley and smiled. "Shall we go?"

Crowley led the way down the wide steps, lit with burning torches. At the bottom, they found themselves in a large open room with nothing but a circle painted on the floor. Aunt Sophia headed for a door at the opposite side. Beyond it, Lux saw another long corridor and more wooden doors.

Lux leaned toward Crowley as they walked down the hall. "Who lights these torches?" he asked.

Crowley grinned. "Dragons."

"Yeah right," said Lux. But when Crowley looked away, Lux glanced behind them.

Aunt Sophia stopped at a door about halfway down the hall and produced an ancient-looking key. Fitting it into the lock, she turned it all the way around three times. The lock gave a faint click.

"After you, dears," she said.

Crowley stepped through with his duffel bag. Lux hurried close on his heels, anxious to see inside.

He found a very comfortable room with a cozy couch and a crackling fire. Shelves lined the room, all packed with books. More books, in waist-high stacks, stood along one wall. Lux walked over to get a closer look. Some of their bindings crumbled to dust at his touch.

These are prehistoric! And I bet one of them has a ritual magic spell to cure Umbra.

A small kitchenette occupied the wall next to the door and in the far corner stood a mahogany screen, carved to look like trees. Behind it, Lux could see the edge of a fluffy feather bed. He recognized the carpet on the stone floor as one his mother discarded the last time she redecorated and the couch and tables looked kind of familiar as well.

"What is this place?" Lux asked.

"It's our ley-over," said Crowley.

54

"Right," said Lux. "Like I know what that means."

"A ley-over is sort of a hotel room, for people traveling the ley network," said Aunt Sophia. Lux took a breath, but she stopped him before he could ask. "I will explain what that is later. Now then, Crowley, do you have all you need?"

He nodded.

"If you've forgotten anything, you can call us. The house phone is on the table. We should be able to shuttle goods through the dumbwaiter during the night, if we need to." She gave him a smile and a hug. "It is very good to have you back, dear."

"It's good to be back," he said. "See you all later! Lux, you take care of all these women. Okay?"

Lux shook his head. "What are you talking about? I thought you were staying here. You're acting like we won't see you. Are you gonna stay down here all the time?"

Crowley just laughed, and promised Lux he would see him soon.

"What do you mean by soon?" he asked. *I am really starting to hate that word.* "Soon like tonight or soon like next week?"

Aunt Sophia pushed Lux toward the door and promised to explain everything upstairs. Lux followed her, still confused. At the top, she sealed the arched opening in the same manner she'd opened it. Lux leaned close, trying to hear the words she spoke.

She's not chanting. She's humming. The same notes over and over: high, low, middle, highest. After a few seconds, the portal shrank away and the more familiar basement appeared around them.

"I don't understand," Lux said the moment the portal was sealed. "Why can't he come up and see us?"

"Upstairs," his aunt directed. "I will explain when we get upstairs."

"I wanted to talk to him." Lux stared at the blank wall. "I had a lot of questions."

"You had questions? Oh my, what a surprise." Aunt Sophia started up the steps.

Lux turned from the wall and followed her. He wanted to know so many things. What were they going to do about Dad? How long is Crowley going to stay down there? Where are the other basements? Are those murderers really going to come to the store? He didn't know if he would ask that last question. He didn't think he wanted to hear the answer.

Chapter Six

Upstairs, Aunt Sophia and Lux found the kitchen in a much nicer state. His mom was stirring something that smelled wonderfully like spaghetti sauce while Leeward Spinnet and Umbra built a card house on the dining room table.

"Everything go all right?" Cerri asked.

"Yes. Very well," Aunt Sophia answered. "There seemed to be very little disturbance. Did you feel anything in the store?"

"No. It was pretty busy though, so maybe I just didn't notice." She turned to Leeward. "Mr. Spinnet, did you sense any energy shifts while we were closing up the store?"

"No, I didn't," he answered.

Lux's mouth dropped. *A coherent answer from Spinnet?*

But then the old man added, "That book was distracting me, flying around outside."

"A flying book?" Cerri asked.

Lux rolled his eyes.

"Yes, it was here again," said Spinnet. "I have it on good authority that books are not allowed to fly, even special books like…what's the word? Altimeter? No, that's not it. Antihistamine? No. Appellate court? Hmm…."

When his aunt went into the kitchen, Lux followed her. "Aunt Sophia?"

"Yes, Lux. As I promised…" She smiled. "What's the first question?"

"Altitude?" said Spinnet from the dining room. "Surely not."

"What are we going to do about Dad?"

Aunt Sophia sighed. "The first question and I don't have an answer for it. Crowley, Cerri and I will have to talk about things. But don't worry, Lux. We won't give up until we have Atlas home."

That made Lux feel some better. "Ok, then why can't Crowley come up?"

"The process of opening the portal to that basement causes a ripple in the energy field of our world." She went to the refrigerator and took out some lettuce. "They're not dangerous, or even very noticeable, but energy ripples are only caused by a few things. Portals, time travel, manifestation and nuclear activity. All of those things are restricted in our country."

She carved the lettuce into wedges and threw it in a big bowl. "Hopefully, no one noticed the slight ripple we caused, but if Crowley were to come and go through the portal many times, it is likely people would notice the shifting energies and report it. Could you get the tomatoes out of the ice box please?"

Lux nodded and searched through the vegetable drawer. As he handed the tomatoes to his aunt, he asked, "What is that place? How come we need a portal to get to it? Why can't we just go down some more stairs?"

"Because that basement is not located below this store. At least not at this moment." She sliced the tomatoes into wedges and tossed them into the salad. "It exists in a separate reality, a moment behind or ahead of us in time, or on a different cosmic plane entirely. No one knows how the old portals work. That knowledge was lost in the Burning Times. We only know that they do work and we use them when we have need. Now the onions please."

Lux fetched the onions. "If they're illegal, who uses them?"

His aunt paused a moment, her knife in the air. "People like us, Lux. People who don't believe that magic is bad."

"How many portals are there?" Lux asked.

"Here in the store, there are several. That's one reason John Pickingill built his shop on this site." His aunt's eyes watered from the onions. "Can you get me a tissue, dear?"

Lux went into the living room and grabbed the box off the end table.

"Armillary?" said Spinnet. "Apiary?"

"Still no luck, Mr. Spinnet?" Lux asked.

"No," he said. "Is it avant-garde?"

"I doubt it," said Lux.

Umbra giggled.

Lux walked into the kitchen and handed the tissue box to his aunt.

"Thank you, Lux," she said. "Now, where were we?"

"Portals."

"Oh yes. Throughout the world, there are thousands of portals. Some we still know of. A great many have been forgotten and haven't been used since before the Burning Times. When portals are not used, they begin to fade and are eventually lost." She continued chopping and sniffling.

"Long ago, there were maps of portal locations; everyone used them. During the Burnings, though, portals became illegal and the maps were dangerous to have around. People destroyed them and so the knowledge was lost." She stared hard at him. "Lux, I don't want you playing at opening any portals. It is too dangerous."

"I won't," he said. But he couldn't help thinking about all the old books in the ley over. *Seems a shame to have all those books down there where nobody reads them.* "You said you would explain the lay network?"

"Yes," she said. "It's spelled 'l-e-y'. You will be studying this in school. To put it simply, ley lines are paths of energy that crisscross the Earth. These

60

paths exist deep in the ground, but some evidence of this energy can be felt here on the crust. Have you ever heard of dowsers?" She scooped the onions into the salad and rinsed her hands.

"No."

"Dowsers are people who have the exceptional ability to sense minute energy shifts. You've probably seen water dowsers, who can locate underground water supplies by walking over an area with two bent rods."

Lux nodded.

"Well, that's one form of dowsing," she said. "In addition to water, dowsers can also sense energy fields, magnetic variances and, as we were discussing, ley lines. Could you put the salad in the ice box?"

Lux crossed the kitchen, mulling over what his aunt had said. "So, ley lines are paths of energy deep in the earth, and dowsers can find them."

His aunt nodded as she dried her hands.

"But what do they do?" he asked.

"The ancient people found that there are points on the earth where these energy paths are closer to the surface. On these points, they built structures of various kinds to channel the energy. Stonehenge is one such structure. Let's go rest a bit, shall we?"

They walked into the dining room and sat down, careful not to bump the table with the card house.

"During the Age of Light," Aunt Sophia continued, "at the height of magical knowledge, the ley network was developed. The network used the ancient portals to gain access to the ley lines, deep underground. Through these lines, people were able to travel anywhere the ley lines went, at great speeds, faster even than our airplanes today."

"Kind of like a subway," Lux said.

"Yes," Aunt Sophia agreed. "Very much like our subways."

"How come I've never heard of them before? Why don't people use them now?" he asked.

"Because..."

But Lux guessed the answer before she even said it. "Illegal?"

"Right," Aunt Sophia replied. "Since portal use was restricted, no one was able to access the ley network. That being the case, the international governments agreed there was no reason to keep the networks open, so everyone stopped using them. Supposedly."

"Supposedly?" asked Lux.

"Adobe?" asked Leeward.

"There are still people using portals, as you know." She smiled. "The ancient sites, Stonehenge and the like, are well tended by those who still follow the Old Ways, and we know from those people that energy still flows along the lines. I think it's a safe bet that ley travel continues to this day. In fact, I know so."

"You do? For a fact?" Lux tried to imagine his prim Aunt Sophia traveling along some energy path at the speed of light.

"I do," she said. "But that's just between you and me. Last question!"

"When will Crowley come back up?"

"Appurtenance?" said Spinnet. "Bah."

"In a week or so, I expect," said Aunt Sophia. "He will let us know when he wants to return."

"How? Through that house phone thing?" Lux remembered the ancient looking telephone that sat on the table.

"Right. Which reminds me...Cerri?" she called. "Your brother would like to have a word with you when you get a chance."

"Sure," she said. "I'll call down after dinner."

Lux wanted to ask more about ley lines, but his aunt went in to help Cerri with the garlic bread. He half listened to Leeward Spinnet as the man continued his word hunt.

"Appendectomy? No. Aspertame? Astronomological?" The old man seemed very frustrated. "No, no, no. What is it?"

"What are you trying to remember, Mr. Spinnet?" Lux asked.

"The word for the book," he answered.

Curiosity got the better of Lux. *Maybe he's trying to say something important we don't understand. Like the other day when he was trying to tell us about Umbra's charm.*

63

Lux waited while Leeward tried out word after word after word. After a long while, Spinnet blurted, "What am I to do with birds that look like books?"

Lux's forehead wrinkled. "What kind of birds look like books?"

"But that's not it, is it? No!" He waved his finger in the air. "No, it's the books that look like birds. That's it. Right then." Satisfied, he went back to building his card tower with Umbra.

"Books that look like birds?" Lux asked.

"Just one today," Spinnet answered.

Lux stared. "Just one what today?"

"Just one bird."

Lux glanced outside. Pigeons perched on the building opposite the store. Several crows sat in the trees below the window. Birds pecked around on the sidewalk and still others flew by.

"Mr. Spinnet, there are a lot of birds out there," Lux said.

"But only one doesn't look like himself, does he? Can't you not see him?"

Lux paused. "I can't...not see him. Can you point him out?"

Leeward looked up. "There's the book, now." He gestured to the balcony, where a lone crow stood pecking in the flower boxes. "You really should invite him in."

"Do what?" Lux asked. "Invite the crow in?"

"No, the book," answered Leeward. "The book. Oh, what's his name? Altitude? Allegory?

Whatever it is, invite him in. That would be best. He would like to come home."

Lux's mouth dropped. *The book! An atlas! That crow is Dad!*

He rushed to the doors and flung them open. But the crow just sat on the railing, looking at him. Lux felt his cheeks redden. *Right. My dad has turned into a crow and is sitting on the balcony, pecking dirt.*

He started to close the door but Leeward shouted, "For Brighid's sake! Where are your manners, boy? Invite the bloody book inside!"

Lux mumbled, "Uh...won't you come inside?" He stepped back to give the crow some room. To his surprise, the crow hopped off the railing and strutted into the dining room.

Now what?

The bird flapped around. Lux looked at Spinnet, who went back to building the card tower. The crow hopped all the way to the kitchen before Cerri spotted it.

"Oh my gosh," she cried. "How did that bird get in here?"

"Not a bird, dear girl," Spinnet corrected. "It's the book. The book what lives here. About time too. He's rather hungry, as am I." He patted his stomach and smiled. "Is it time for dinner?"

Cerri looked at him and then at Lux, who still stood next to the open door.

"Well..." said Lux. "Mr. Spinnet said...could that bird be Dad?"

Cerri raised her eyebrows.

Aunt Sophia looked hard at the bird. "Great Scott! He's right! Cerri, it's Atlas!"

"That's it. Atlas! I knew it would come to me." Leeward yelled. He leaned down to speak to the bird. "Welcome home, son."

Lux rushed into the kitchen, right behind the crow. "Is that really Dad?"

Cerri shrugged. Aunt Sophia cleared the plates and silverware off the kitchen table.

"Who turned him into a crow?" Lux demanded.

"I imagine he did it himself," said Aunt Sophia. "To escape the tunnels."

"Then why doesn't he change himself back?" said Lux.

"How?" said Cerri. "Using his wings to mix up the counter-tonic?"

"Oh, right," said Lux.

"Put him up here," said Aunt Sophia. "We'll need to attempt a reversal."

Lux picked up the crow, cradling it in his hands. It made no sound or movement as he sat it on the table. Everyone crowded around. Aunt Sophia collected candles, herbs, salt and small dishes. A mountain of stuff grew on the table next to the crow. Then Aunt Sophia ordered everyone except Cerri out of the apartment.

Leeward Spinnet ushered them downstairs to the store, where they waited. Lux paced back and forth. Umbra hopped up and down on the squeaky third step, waiting for the door to open at the top. Only Spinnet seemed unaffected. He sat on a bench in one of the dressing rooms trying to create crystal-light between two pieces of quartz.

It's been two hours! When are they going to be done? Lux's stomach growled so loudly he knew everyone could hear it.

"Mr. Spinnet. Can we order a pizza or something?"

"Pizza?" said the old man. "Certainly! I've always loved pizza. I like mine with baked beans and crushed aspirin. And a glass of prune juice."

I guess that means I have to call.

Lux dug the phone book out and dialed the number for Margaret's Italian Palace. Half an hour later, they were gorging themselves on pineapple pizza and soda. (Margaret's didn't carry prune juice.) Their stomachs full, they resumed their anxious waiting.

At close to ten o'clock, Cerri called them upstairs. All three rushed for the steps, creating a scrum at the door. Lux tripped over Umbra and hit the door frame. "Ouch."

In the kitchen, they found Atlas drinking coffee at the table.

"Dad!" Lux threw himself on his father. Umbra followed close on his heels.

Everyone talked all at once, so loud they couldn't hear each other. Spinnet pulled a chair into the corner and stared at them.

Lux went over to him. "What's wrong, Mr. Spinnet?"

"Wrong?" He shook his wild gray hair. "Nothing. Not one single thing."

"Then why are you sitting here alone?" said Lux.

"My dear boy." He patted Lux's arm. "I'm just admiring the view."

Chapter Seven

The Pickingills and St. Clares stayed up very late that night. While Cerri and Aunt Sophia explained, as best they could, Umbra's invisibility, Lux fired questions at his father faster than Atlas could answer them.

"Were you in those tunnels? How did you escape? Are those murderers going to come after you? How did you turn into a crow?"

Cerri called down to the ley-over to let Crowley know about Atlas's return. "He said he was heading straight to the Ramsbottom to let everyone at the pub know."

"Hang on," said Lux. "Dad's kidnapping was a secret from me and Umbra, but the rest of world knew all about it?"

"You are correct, sir," said Spinnet.

Margaret's Italian Palace made its second delivery of the night, and between bites of pizza, Atlas told his family what had happened.

"A few days before I left," Atlas began, "we received word from our spies that Sprenger was planning to blow up the ley network."

"We have spies?" said Lux.

His mother shushed him. "Let your father talk." She picked up the remote and muted the TV.

Atlas continued. "I organized several groups to patrol the network. Crowley and I headed for the main terminal. We felt vibrations as soon as we got there. I didn't know what it was, but figured it must be Sprengers doing and followed the sound several miles through the maintenance walkways.

"We got there, literally, in the nick of time. The driller had just broken through the obsidian crust of the ley line, and energy was beginning to seep out. It melted the driller in about a minute. Sprenger's men ran. The breach wasn't huge, but it was leaking enough energy to destroy whatever was above it in a matter of hours."

"The ley lines can melt stuff?" said Lux. "Wicked."

"Wicked is right," his father said. "It could have dissolved half the city if we hadn't been there. Crowley ran back to the terminal and told the ley operators to block off that section and divert the energy flow. I started plugging the breach with chunks of obsidian. The leakage stopped, so I headed back to the terminal. About halfway, I ran into Sprenger's men and they delivered me right into his hands."

70

Cerri shuddered. Leeward Spinnet spat into the fire. Even Atlas looked a little pale.

"Needless to say, Sprenger was thrilled to see me. He gave me a nice accommodation in the honeymoon suite. No view but the food was...well, there was no food." Lux's father gave a hollow laugh. "Lucky for me, they didn't take my coat. I was able to find enough bits and pieces in my pockets to cobble together a transmutation spell. Once the moon cycled around, I turned myself into a crow and flew the coop. Nice place, the tunnels, but you wouldn't want to live there."

Lux tried to imagine the tunnels, but he doubted his imagination did them justice. *And Dad might still be there, if it hadn't been for some stuff in his pockets and the spell he knew.* "Dad, was that spell, the one where you turned into a crow, was that ritual magic?"

Aunt Sophia's eyes darted toward him.

Atlas shook his head. "Oh, no. Ritual magic is illegal. I don't know anyone who would attempt it these days. Too risky."

He turned to Cerri. "How are things here, my favorite girl? The store is running ok, I assume?"

Lux stared at the television as they talked. *Too risky? If Dad wouldn't use ritual magic to escape from Sprenger, does it really make sense to use it on Umbra? She's not in nearly as much danger as he was. Besides, Dad might know how to fix Umbra. There are probably lots of things Aunt Sophia and Mom haven't thought of.*

71

As Lux tried to convince himself of that, the television screen went blank then flickered back on to read "Breaking News". Toffee Baxter, the anchor woman, sat ruffling papers as the camera closed in on her. The small screen to the right of her head showed a group of people scuffling with Inquisitors below the words "Wiccean Arrests".

"Where's the remote?" his father asked. "Turn that up, Cerri. I want to hear…"

Toffee's voice filled the room. *"…clashed with Wiccean protestors tonight in front of the Capitol building, resulting in seven arrests. The Inquisitors maintain the protestors attacked them with balls of fire and--"* Toffee glanced off to the side, as if questioning what she read. *"--and shadow warriors?"*

"Shadow what?" said Lux.

"The area around the Capitol has been closed to all traffic. Police and Inquisitors are working together to get the situation under control and hope to have the building open for business tomorrow morning. They ask that people please avoid the area until further notice. Stay tuned to Channel Six for updates on this and any other breaking news stories." Toffee gave a half-hearted smile then stood up and walked off camera.

Lux heard her say, "What, in the name of Cerrnunos, is a shadow warrior?" before they cut to commercial.

"Good question," he said. "What is a shadow warrior?"

"Nonsense, is what it is." His father looked as if he didn't know whether to laugh or scream. "Fire throwers? Phoenix Jetson is the only fire thrower left in the country and he must be ninety years old. He couldn't throw a tennis ball, much less a fire ball."

Cerri's dark eyes remained fixed on the screen. "This is bad. They've actually arrested Wicceans, on television no less. And for what? Trumped up charges. Flat out lies."

"Trumpets and flies," cried Spinnet. He shook his finger at the television. "Trumpets and flies. You mark my words, this is the beginning."

Atlas nodded. "The beginning of the end."

"The end?" Leeward snorted. "You'll wish it was the end by the time it's over. No sir, this is the beginning of the beginning." He picked up a bag of marshmallows and sank into the bean bag chair near the fireplace mumbling, "Crumpets and pies."

"You're probably right, Leeward," Atlas said. "But there's nothing to be done tonight." He switched off the TV and looked at his watch. "It's late. You kids should be in bed."

Lux complained all the way up the stairs. "I haven't seen Dad in forever! Why can't I stay up another hour?"

"Because you have school," said his mother and father together.

"This is so unfair," Lux said. He went to his room and put on his pajamas. Then he opened his door and crept back down the stairway. He stifled a yelp as he tripped over something on the landing.

"Umbra?"

One squeeze.

Even she knows the best information comes out after they think we're in bed.

Umbra tapped his hand again, as if she agreed. They sat just behind the wall on the last step and listened, unseen from the living room.

"Sprenger has shifted his search into high gear," said his father.

"His search for what?" Aunt Sophia asked.

"We still aren't sure," Atlas said. "We assume he's looking for one of the Tools of Legend. The question is which one."

Tools of Legend? Why would Sprenger be looking for some ancient, magic tools? Weren't they all created to protect the Wiccae?

"My best guess," his father said, "is that he's looking for the Iron Bodkin."

"The Bodkin?" said Cerri. "That doesn't seem likely. There's no proof it was ever actually created."

"It was written about all through the Burning Times," said Aunt Sophia.

"Lots of things were written about in the Burning Times," Cerri argued. "Just because there were rumors about the Church hiring warlocks to craft a spike that removes witches' powers doesn't mean they actually did it."

"There's no real proof that any of the Tools of Legend existed, much less still exist," said Atlas. "For my part, I think Sprenger wants the Bodkin. After all, a spike that removes a witch's power? What could be more dangerous in his hands?"

"The Rutilus Sardonyx," Aunt Sophia replied.

Lux's eyes grew wide and Umbra drew in a quick breath. The Rutilus Sardonyx--The Red Tools--the stuff of campfire stories. Lux pictured the tools in his mind: Five enormous rubies, each carved with intricate symbols, forming the handles of five different tools.

"Did you know they've been kept by the same family for thousands of years?" he whispered to Umbra. "That's how the first five craft families got their magic. Each tool gave a different power. Before that, there was magic, but nobody could shape-shift, vanish, teleport, tell the future or do mind control. I wish the St. Clares had--"

Umbra shushed him with an elbow to his ribs.

"Ow."

"I don't know, Sophia," his father said. "What makes you think Sprenger is looking for the Red Gems? Why would he waste so much time trying to find something that provides magic?"

"As long as the tools exist, magic can never be purged from this world," she said.

"I suppose that's true," said Atlas. "Well, whatever Sprenger's looking for, he's doubled the number of men searching, as well as the number of places being searched. The word from Europe is that the caves in France and Spain, as well as the dolmen sites in Great Britain, are all being targeted. Sprenger is working round the clock; it's as if he has a deadline. Any thoughts on what that may mean?"

"None," said Cerri.

"Nor me," said his aunt. "But I will certainly check my sources. And I'll confer with Leeward tomorrow. I hate to wake him up right now."

"No, let him sleep," said Cerri. "He had quite a day running the store."

"Great man, Leeward. I don't know what we'd do without him." His father's voice held no trace of irony.

The couch springs squeaked. Lux pulled back from the edge of the landing.

"I'm afraid I'm going to have to go to bed," said Atlas. "I haven't gotten a decent night's sleep in eons. You can't imagine how hard it is to balance on those electrical wires."

Lux and Umbra crept up the stairs to their bedrooms. Lux eased his door shut and climbed into bed as Atlas's footsteps thudded past. Lux smiled at the familiar sound, but worry still wriggled through his gut.

Nothing's fixed, after all. Umbra's still invisible, my friends still aren't speaking to me and from the looks of the news, Inquisitors have started arresting innocent people. That's the last thing we need, with Umbra breaking the law and Dad and Crowley hiding from Sprenger. The question is, what are we going to do about it all?

Chapter Eight

Morning came very early for Lux. He sat at the breakfast table and slopped cereal down his shirt.

"Mom, can't I just stay home today?" he begged. There was no way he was going to stay awake in class and, as usual, none of his homework was done.

"I'm sorry, but you have to go, Lux." She yawned. "Umbra's been out for a week now. If you don't go, I'm afraid the school will send someone to check on her."

Great. I can't even take a sick day with Umbra invisible.

Through the balcony doors, he saw the bus rolling along Fort Street. He grabbed his bag and stumbled down the stairs to the alley. As soon as the bus started moving, he fell asleep.

Lux spent lunchtime catching up with Cyril, who had used his sick days to create a tonic that made his hair glow in the dark. It worked well, but also turned his hair salmon pink so they spent the better part of lunch pouring through his herbal encyclopedia, looking for a counter tonic.

"This might work." Cyril pointed to a recipe. "A restorative paste."

"That's the same recipe mom and Aunt Sophia tried on Umb..." Lux stopped himself just in time.

"On Umbra?" asked Cyril.

"Nothing," said Lux.

Cyril frowned. "You can tell me."

"It was nothing." Lux changed the subject. "I think the potion might work for you."

"Maybe we can brew it this weekend," said Cyril.

Lux shrugged. "Maybe." *But probably not since my sister is invisible and Inquisitors are roaming the streets.*

When the final bell of the day rang, Lux sighed with relief. He threw his books into his locker and raced to the bus zone. Cyril caught up with him as he boarded the bus.

"Hey Lux! My mom says you can spend the night tonight. We rented Architecture of the Ancients and The Baths of Pompeii." Cyril planned to be an architect like his mom. "Do you think your parents will let you come over? I'm not sick anymore."

"Umm...I don't think I can. My dad's been away...on business. He just got back last night," Lux answered, telling as much of the truth as he dared. "I probably ought to hang out at home tonight."

"Oh. Okay," said Cyril. "Well, how about if I come over there? I can bring the movies."

"No!" Lux said. "I mean, I don't think it would be a good idea. My mom kind of wants it to be just family for my dad's first night back."

"Oh....fine. Whatever." Cyril's smile fell away and he opted to share a seat with Emily Sutton instead of sitting in the single seat across from Lux.

Great. Now even Cyril's mad at me...all because Umbra's invisible. And it's never going to change since there doesn't seem to be a cure for her.

Well...there is a cure. Lux pushed the thought away. *If ritual magic was too risky for Dad, it must be seriously dangerous. We'll have to find some other way to fix Umbra. Of course, I don't have any friends left anyway, so maybe it doesn't matter.*

By the time he got home, Lux had worked himself into quite a funk and wanted to talk his problems over with his father. He turned the corner and stumbled over Crowley, who sat on the steps outside the store.

"Whoa! Sorry," Lux said.

"Ouch, man. Watch where you're going." They sorted themselves out. Crowley held out his fist, which Lux tapped with his own. "What's going on in the world of Pickingill Elementary these days?"

"Observation and Calibration."

His uncle groaned. "I remember that class being the worst of many."

"It's still bad," Lux replied.

"Does Madame Skellis teach it?"

"No," said Lux. "I think she died. We have Master Bortuga."

"Ah, well, Madame Skellis was about a thousand-and-five when I had her. I guess she lived a full life." He held up his soda. "To Madame Skellis." He took a long gulp.

"What are you doing out of the basement?" Lux asked.

"Things have changed, haven't they?" Crowley grinned. "Before, we were trying not to attract attention so we could get your dad back. Now that he is, he wants all hands on deck in case the Inquisitors try anything.

"Of course, Sprenger wouldn't attempt anything on us with your Dad back in the public eye. They're on the same side, you know."

"Yeah, right," scoffed Lux. "I read the papers a lot when you guys were gone. I know Sprenger is against the Wiccae."

"Good call. Anyway, I wanted to see Atlas. It's good to have him home," Crowley smiled.

"No kidding." Lux stood up. "I'm going to talk to him right now."

"Sorry bud, you'll have to wait. He went into the office this morning and won't be home for another few hours."

"He went to work?" Lux's shoulders slumped. "He said he was just going to rest for a couple days."

Crowley laughed. "Yeah—then he saw the morning news and realized how much anti-magic legislation the Ordinaricans introduced while he was gone. I'm glad I wasn't in their shoes this morning. He was furious when he left!"

"He's always furious about the Ordinaricans," said Lux. "They've been trying to outlaw magic forever."

Crowley nodded. "And still trying."

Lux rubbed his head.

"What's wrong, dude?" his uncle asked. "You look really down."

Lux sat on the step next to Crowley. "I'm sick of Umbra being invisible. I want our life to go back to the way it used to be. I can't have any of my friends over; I can't tell them why, and now they're all mad at me."

"All of them?" Crowley asked.

"Yes," Lux said. "Every one--even Cyril, and he's my best friend. Usually I tell him everything. It's not fair."

"No, it's not fair, but you can't tell him, Lux," said Crowley.

Lux scowled.

"You know all those questions you keep asking, and your mom and AnSo keep saying you're not old enough? Well, this is part of it. If you're old enough to know what's going on with Umbra and Atlas, then you've got to deal with not telling anyone.

It's not always fun being grown up. In fact, a lot of the time it stinks."

"Great," Lux grumbled. "Something to look forward to."

Crowley patted him on the back. "I bet Cyril will get over it. Maybe you guys could do something this weekend. As long as it's not here, I don't think Cerri would mind. How 'bout if I drive you to the skate park?"

"Really?" Lux's spirits lifted a bit. "That'd be cool. I'll go ask mom."

"I'll come with you. It's stone boring out here."

They climbed the steps and walked into the shop. The bell tinkled and Lux breathed in the scent of Pickingill's Magical Notions. Incense and dust, old wood and lemon oil smelled like home to him. His mom stood behind the counter, talking to three of her regular customers.

"Hi sweetheart! How was school?" she said.

Ugh. Sweetheart? "Good," said Lux. "Crowley said he'd take me and Cyril to the skate park this weekend if it's ok with you. Can I go?"

"Sure," said Cerri. "You haven't seen much of Cyril lately."

"I know," Lux said. "I'm gonna call him."

He ran through the store and up the stairs. In the dining room, he found Aunt Sophia and Leeward Spinnet playing Go-Fish with Umbra, whose cards floated across the table from them.

"Well, look who's home," his aunt said. "What's the rush?"

"I'm going to call Cyril to see if he can go to the skate park with me and Crowley," Lux said.

"Crowley and me," his aunt corrected.

"Me too!" said Leeward. "I do love skating."

Umbra laughed. Lux imagined Spinnet on a skateboard wearing his striped running tights and red fake-fur coat and laughed too. Aunt Sophia seemed to realize Spinnet was the butt of their joke and glared.

Lux headed for the phone and dialed Cyril's number. His friend answered.

"Hey, Cyril. It's Lux."

Silence.

This is going to be harder than I thought.

"Um, I talked to my mom about this weekend...about us maybe doing something?"

Silence.

"Cyril? Are you there?"

"I'm here," a sullen voice answered.

"Oh. Okay...well, Crowley said he'd take us to the skate park sometime. My mom said it was okay," Lux waited for some response, but none came. "So, do you want to go?"

Silence.

Lux sighed. "Look, I'm really sorry I can't do anything tonight. It's just that my Dad's been gone for so long, and I want to see him."

More silence.

Lux waited a moment longer, and then gave up. "Well, if you change your mind, I guess we'll go Saturday morning sometime. Bye."

Lux made his way back to the living room, more depressed than ever. *I knew Cy was mad, but I didn't think he was that mad.*

He walked over to the balcony doors, then froze with his hand on the door knob. Two Inquisitors stood on the opposite side of the street, staring at the store. His stomach lurched.

What are they doing? Are they coming to get Umbra? Looking for Dad?

His heart pounded as he watched the Inquisitors. After a nervous minute and several hiccups from Lux, the Inquisitors moved up the street. He turned away from the door and bumped into something solid where there seemed to be nothing at all.

"Umbra?"

She took his hand and squeezed. Then she tapped the window. He glanced up. The Inquisitors stood halfway down the block, still watching.

"You saw them too?" he whispered. One squeeze. "Don't worry. They weren't here for you." *Two squeezes. Umbra doesn't believe me.*

"Are you scared?" he asked. After a long pause, she squeezed once. Lux squeezed back.

I don't blame her. If Inquisitors keep watching Dad, they'll find out about her eventually. And after

*seeing them arresting people last night, I'm sure they'd
arrest someone for being invisible--even if she is only six.*

*This is stupid. If they're going to arrest people who
aren't doing anything wrong, why bother doing anything
right? Ritual magic doesn't seem like much of a risk, when
people are going to jail for carrying signs at the Capitol.*

Lux dropped his fist on the window sill. *I'll do
it. I'll find a spell and I'll fix Umbra. Now, I just have to
find the spell...*

The kitchen door opened and voices drifted
into the living room. Aunt Sophia and Spinnet stood
up from their card game as Crowley, Cerri and Atlas
walked in.

"Dad," said Lux. "You're home."

"Yes, I am." Atlas grinned. "I intend to make
coming home a regular thing. In fact, I might even do
it every day."

Everyone laughed. Lux gave a half smile, still
thinking about the Inquisitors.

"I closed the store early," Cerri said. "I
thought we needed to have some family time."

"Great," said Atlas. "I have some things I want
to talk about, and it's good that everyone is here."

Lux sat down on the floor near the fireplace.
From there, he could peek through the titles, looking
for anything on Ritual Magic. Everyone else took
seats as Atlas opened his briefcase and pulled out a
folder.

"The Inquisitorial Corps has been given
permission to patrol the streets, which means they

can go wherever they like and do whatever they deem necessary to 'keep the peace'. Since the store is a public place, they can come in anytime."

Lux stopped his search to stare at his father. "Seriously? Inquisitors can come in the store?"

Atlas nodded. "Sadly yes, which means, we need to do something about Umbra." He tapped the folder he was holding. "I talked to an old friend of mine who runs a boarding school in New York. She has agreed to issue a Certificate of Enrollment for Umbra that we can show the Board of Education here."

Lux raised his eyebrows. "Umbra's going to live in New York?" Umbra squeezed his arm very tight. "I don't think she wants to."

His mom reached over and patted Umbra. "She's not going anywhere. The school in New York won't actually list her as a student, and the Certificate will keep the school here from checking on her."

"Then where's she going to go to school?" Lux asked.

"I'll take over Umbra's education," said Aunt Sophia. "She'll stay here at home and we'll have school during the day." His aunt tried to look pleased, but she couldn't hide the discouragement in her voice.

"Umbra's just going to stay invisible and never leave the house?" Lux asked. "Very bad idea!"

"Well," Cerri said. "Not never. I mean, we should be able to go to the park sometimes. And maybe the zoo, if it's not too crowded."

Lux couldn't believe it. His parents wanted to leave things the way they were? *Umbra can't live her whole life stuck in the house. What if she gets sick and needs a doctor? What about friends? What about college? And what about me? I'm not gonna have any friends over for the rest of my life?* He turned to the bookcase and resumed his search for a book on Ritual Magic.

"Right then," his father said. "That's settled. The other thing I wanted to talk about was magic training."

Lux whipped around to face his dad once again. "Whose magic training?"

"Yours and Umbra's. We've waited too long and now it looks like things are going to get...well, get worse," said his father. "You need to know how to take care of yourselves if anything ever happens." He pulled two thick books out of his briefcase. They were bound in new red leather with the words "Beginning Magical Instruction" printed along the spine. "Leeward will be training you."

Lux choked back a snort as his father handed he and Umbra each a book.

This has gotta be a joke. Spinnet teaching us magic? Umbra never leaving the house? Any second, Dad'll say he's teasing and we'll all have a good laugh.

"Crowley, do you have a minute," said Atlas. "I wanted to talk to you about something." They sat down on the couch and started talking politics.

So that's it? Here's a book, your sister has to stay invisible? Lux thumbed through the new book and wondered if it taught ritual magic. It didn't.

How to grind roots. Chants for happiness. Proper sweeping techniques? Ugh! Baby Magic 101. Lux shoved it under the couch, and pulled a book off the shelf called 'Special Tonics and Protective Potions'.

"There's new legislation being pushed through the Senate, championed by none other than our own Vice-President Kramer," his father said to Crowley. "It requires all children born to a magical parent to be registered."

"That's insane," said Crowley. "That would be hundreds of thousands of kids a year. How are they going to do that? And why? Magical parents don't always have magical kids."

"To create their long dreamt of 'black list'," said Atlas. "Once these registered kids grow up, they'll be discriminated against at every turn. Last on the college enrollment lists, first in line for income tax audits. The government will scrutinize their every move."

Umbra wandered off as Lux scanned page after page of tonics and elixirs. At the end, he found the same recipe for huckleberry tea they had tried on Umbra last week. He sighed and slammed the book.

This is stupid. If Mom and Dad have books on ritual magic, they're not going to keep them in the living room. They'd hide them somewhere...like down in the ley-over.

"Why is the Vice-President in favor of it?" Crowley asked.

"I believe Vice President Kramer has his own agenda—and it has nothing to do with the Paritists," said his father.

The ley-over would be the perfect hiding place. You have to be magic to get there, which means Inquisitors could never find them.

He stood up and walked over to the window. The Inquisitors still watched the store, this time from the next block up.

I have to get into the ley-over. Tonight. I can't wait any longer, not with Inquisitors watching us 24/7. If I can just figure out how to open the portal.

Humming under his breath, he tried to remember the tones Aunt Sophia used.

"What does that mean? You think he's switching allegiances?" Crowley asked.

"No," his father said. "I think his true allegiances are just beginning to show."

"But he's been with the Paritist party for years," Crowley said. "Are you saying he's been faking it all this time? You think he's actually working for the Ord's?"

Lux's attention drifted to what his father and Crowley talked about. He leaned toward the couch and tried to catch their words.

"When is the time for pumpkin pie?" asked Spinnet.

"Worse," Atlas said. "I think he's actually working for..." He whispered the last word.

"No way!" said Crowley.

"Who?" said Lux.

"When are we going to eat?" cried Spinnet.

Then, in the silence that followed, a strange voice filled the room--a girl's voice, strong and resonant. She spoke very slow and uttered words which made no sense to Lux.

"He comes on the morrow, with many in tow, seeking destruction of those who know."

Cerri gasped and covered her mouth. After a moment, Lux realized Umbra had spoken the words. Umbra, who had never spoken in her life. Atlas and Crowley sat with their mouths hanging open.

"No pie for me, thanks," mumbled Spinnet. He sat down on the couch, trembling.

Aunt Sophia's face paled as she made her way toward Umbra's voice. With her arms out, she groped through thin air until she found her.

"Come here, dear." She led Umbra to the rocking chair and lifted her onto her lap. They rocked in the quiet room. No one seemed ready to talk about what happened. They sat in silence for an eternity. At last, Lux could stand it no more.

"Uh…what was that?" he asked.

Spinnet offered the answer. "Foretelling."

Chapter Nine

"Foretelling? It can't be," his mother said. "Umbra won't have that gift. She's a St. Clare."

"What else could it be, Cerri?" Aunt Sophia asked.

"A foretelling about what?" Lux asked.

Crowley snorted. "All foretellings are about the future."

"I know that," Lux snapped. "But what did it mean?"

"It cannot be a foretelling," his mother insisted. "Umbra's name is St. Clare. She'll have the power of mind control, or nothing at all."

"Yes." Spinnet nodded. "Or one of Two."

"What does that mean?" Lux asked. "One of two what?"

Crowely frowned.

Cerri threw up her hands. "It was not a foretelling!" she cried. "And Umbra is not one of the Two, for Brighid's sake!"

"Oh." Crowley's eyebrows flew up.

"Crowley, what's the Two?" Lux whispered.

"The Legend of the Two," his uncle whispered back. "Haven't you ever heard it?"

Lux shook his head.

"The legend says that in times of great distress, a pair of Wiccaes will be united. Between them, they will bear all five of the original craft talents, and they will turn the tide of energy for the good of the craft."

"Wow," Lux said. "And they think Umbra is one of them?"

Crowley nodded.

"Why?" asked Lux.

"Because she just issued a foretelling, which she shouldn't be able to do. Her name is St. Clare, so she shouldn't have any gifts other than mind control. Spinnet thinks, since she has a gift she shouldn't have, maybe she's one of the Two."

Lux wrinkled his nose. Umbra? The fulfillment of a legend? "That's crazy."

Crowley shrugged.

Of course, Umbra just spoke for the first time in her life, to make a prediction. I guess her being one of the Two makes as much sense as anything else.

"Foretelling or not," said Atlas, "we need to treat Umbra's words as a warning. We need to prepare as if something is going to happen tomorrow;

94

something apparently detrimental to the craft. I think we should gather the Covens."

Lux sat up straight. "There hasn't been a Gathering since before I was born."

"Or me," said Crowley.

"Can you call a Gathering?" Lux asked his dad.

"Of course. Any Wiccae can call a Gathering." Atlas turned to Cerri. "What's the moon phase?"

"Waxing, between the first quarter and full," she said.

"Good, we can work with that," said Atlas. "Crowley, I want you to alert the elders of every coven. Let them know what's happened. We'll gather tomorrow evening on the Serpent Mounds."

"You got it." Crowley left the room at a jog and grabbed his backpack on the way out.

"Cerri," Atlas continued, "I want you to take the kids and go to Sophia's house. I don't--"

"What?" Lux cried. "No way! I'm going to the Gathering."

"No, Lux," said Atlas. "I have no idea what we'll run into. If Inquisitors show up, I don't want Umbra anywhere near them."

"But I'm not invisible!" said Lux. "Why can't I go?"

"I'm not going to argue with you," said his father. "Cerri, you can take them out to the farm first thing in the morning. Whatever happens, you'll be safer there than in the store."

"In the morning? What about school?" said Lux.

"You'll have to miss a day," said Atlas. "You and Umbra should pack a few things; you may be there the rest of the weekend." Lux opened his mouth again, but his father cut him off. "No arguing!"

Lux stomped up the stairs. *This is so not fair!* He stormed into his room and slammed the door.

Fine. If I can't go to the Gathering, I can at least make sure it's the last thing I miss because of Umbra. I'm going to the ley-over tonight. I'll have all night to look through the books and find the spell I need.

Lux laid on his bed and practiced the portal chant until his father poked his head in.

"I'm sorry I yelled at you Lux."

Lux nodded.

"I want to make sure you understand what's going on."

Lux wriggled up as Atlas sat on the edge of his bed.

"Strictly speaking, there is no way Umbra could have issued a foretelling. She carries the St. Clare name, and the St. Clare's were only given the gift of mind control. On the other hand, Umbra has clearly issued a foretelling. So..." He shrugged. "There we are."

"What did the foretelling mean?" Lux asked. "What's going to happen?"

"Foretelling is never an exact science. When one is issued, people don't usually know what it means until after it comes true," his father said. "But if you want my best guess, I think it means Sprenger and the MM are planning some type of attack on the Wiccae community."

Lux sucked in a breath. "Murklin's Murderers?"

Atlas raised one eyebrow. "Where did you learn about 'Murklin's Murderers'?"

Lux didn't want to get his uncle in trouble. "Just around."

"Around?" his father asked. "Around Crowley, I suppose." Lux nodded. "It's time you started learning about these things, but I want you to learn facts, not rumors. The MM does not stand for 'Murklin's Murderers'. It's a secret society, so no one knows for sure, but some believe it stands for Malleus Malificarum."

Lux shivered.

"Does that name mean anything to you?" his father asked.

"No," Lux said. "It just sounds kind of spooky."

"It should. The Malleus Malificarum was a treatise, a sort of book, written during the Burning Times. It was used by Inquisitors as a manual of how to determine whether or not a person was a witch, and what to do with them if they were. It was a horrible, violent piece of writing." His father's voice quivered and Lux wondered what, exactly, the book said to do with the witches.

"When the Burning Times ended, the books fell by the wayside. But there were still those who refused to accept wiccaes or magic as part of their world. Those people banded together to form a secret society, committed to stamping out magic. That group has persevered through the ages, destroying the Old Ways however they could. We believe that group, the MM, has taken their initials from the original witch hunting handbook, the Malleus Malificarum.

His father sighed. "There's so much for you two to learn, but we don't have time now. You wanted to know about Umbra's prophecy."

Lux nodded.

"Her words were, 'He comes on the morrow, with many in tow, seeking destruction of those who know'. What do you think that might mean?"

"Well," said Lux. "I think the 'he' means Sprenger. And the 'many in tow', I guess that means his army...the MM?"

"Yes, that's right in line with how I interpreted it. What about the rest? What about 'those who know'?"

Lux thought. He hadn't understood that part at all, but given what he'd just learned... "Maybe he means people who know about the MM?"

"That's a possibility," said Atlas. "I think 'those who know' refers to the Wiccae, in general.

We've always been called 'wise' or 'those of knowledge'. And Sprenger certainly would like to bring destruction to us. But, that's just my guess, and yours is as good as mine, at this point." His father pulled him into a bear hug. "I really missed you," he said. "When this is over, we have a lot of work to do. We've held off far too long in your craft training."

Lux wanted to ask what kind of training they would have, but Aunt Sophia called Atlas downstairs. With nothing to do but wait until everyone went to bed, Lux headed down to watch TV.

"Lux," said his mom. "Can you get yourself and Umbra something to eat?" She sat at her desk, checking the moon and planet charts in the newspaper. "I need to finish these calculations."

"Sure," said Lux. He went into the kitchen.

A spoon hovered in the air then dipped down into a jar of peanut butter.

"Is that what you want for dinner?" he asked his sister.

She tapped the spoon once on the side of the jar then dipped it in again.

"I'll have that too." He pulled another spoon out of the drawer and dug in.

After eating their fill of peanut butter, they split an apple, polished off a bag of cookies and topped it off by eating ice cream out of the carton and drizzling chocolate syrup into their mouths. In Umbra's case, the chocolate dripped out of the bottle then disappeared into thin air.

99

An hour later, Aunt Sophia and Spinnet walked through the kitchen with Atlas on their way out.

"Your work will be crucial, as usual," Atlas told them. "Any information you can give us may make the difference."

"Of course," his aunt said. "We'll meditate on the signs and Leeward can read the energies. We'll meet you on the mounds tomorrow before the circle is cast."

Leeward bowed to Atlas then looked him in the eye and said, "The winner shall prevail."

Atlas closed the door behind them, and turned to Lux and Umbra. "Lux, you need to get to bed. Umbra, you too," he added as the chocolate bottle floated toward the refrigerator. "You'll need to be up early tomorrow to go to the farm."

Lux didn't argue. *The sooner everyone goes to bed, the sooner I can head down to the portal.* As he climbed the stairs, he heard Umbra's soft steps behind him. He pushed open his door and mumbled, "G'night, Umbra."

Lux gasped as she threw her arms around him. "Whoa! What's that for?"

Umbra took his hand and squeezed three times. She went into her room and closed the door. *Three squeezes? What does that mean?*

He lied down on his bed and waited for his parents to go to sleep.

Chapter Ten

Around midnight, Atlas and Cerri came upstairs. Lux waited another half hour, peeked through the hall and checked to make sure no light shone under his parent's door.

He crept through the house and down the stairway to the basement. Lux faced the blank stone wall and concentrated on his memory of Aunt Sophia opening the portal. As he held his hand out, he felt a tingling in his palm. *It's working!*

He chanted the notes, long and slow. A river of warmth flowed up his arm. The middle of the wall glowed a dull orange but soon faded.

Lux gave it another try. His arm grew warm, but again it didn't last and the wall stood just as solid as ever. "C'mon, I know I can do this."

Once more, he extended his hand. *Clear your brain. Think about the notes.* He held each tone until it vibrated through his head and his ears rang with the sound. His eyes closed in concentration.

The books are on the other side. I have to get through. I can see the archway. I'm walking through it. I need those books!

At last, a thick, warm ripple coursed through his body. He opened his eyes. The stone wall had disappeared and an open archway led to a stairway.

"Wow." He smiled. "I actually did it."

Lux started down the steps and glanced over his shoulder, wondering if he should close the portal. Instead, he crossed the empty room and opened the door on the other side. "With my luck, I'd get stuck down here forever if I closed it."

After two more stairways, Lux reached the door of the ley-over. He twisted the knob but it didn't move.

"Oh no! Aunt Sophia had a key." He shook the door and gave it a good kick, but it didn't budge. "Why didn't I think about that?"

Lux slid down and sat on the welcome mat. He banged his head against the wood, thinking of the books on the other side.

"Well, I can't give up." He reached up and tried the knob again. "It might be years before I get another chance to come down here, and I might not be able to open the portal again. Maybe I can pick the lock."

He searched the ground for a piece of wire or metal. He saw nothing but the welcome mat with curly letters that spelled out 'Cead Mile Failte'.

'A hundred thousand welcomes'…just like the mat at Six Mile Farm.

Aunt Sophia's welcome mat moved around as the front door changed locations, but wherever it ended up, Lux and Umbra knew it always hid a key underneath, in case they needed to get into the house.

Of course! Lux leapt up and flung back the mat. On the stone cobbles lay a large, brass key, just like the one Aunt Sophia used. He snatched it up and inserted it into the lock. He spun it around three times and heard a faint click.

Sweet!

Lux opened the door and stepped into the ley-over. No fire warmed the room and he rubbed his arms against the chill. The lights worked fine though, and Lux dove into the first stack of books. Old bindings crumbled at his touch. Languages he couldn't read stared back at him. He peered at titles and thumbed through indexes. *Potions of the Dark. A Compendium of Extinct Plants.*

He sucked in his breath. "Oh. My. Gosh. *Poisonous Herbs and How to Grow Them*. This is better than Christmas!"

For hours, he searched and sorted. He made a stack of books he wanted to take up to his room, a stack for Umbra and even a couple for Cyril. The rest he put in neat columns. Five books contained spells that looked promising, but Lux's eyes were getting dry and tired.

Maybe I'll take these five and go back. It's gotta be getting late. He sat an armful of books on top of a tall stack, which then crashed to the floor.

"Ugh!" Weary, Lux bent to clean up the mess and noticed a book that had been wedged behind the toppled stack. Covered in tattered black silk, the title read *Anchient Spelles and Soursouries.* Lux picked it up and thumbed through it. Like most of the older books, it contained no index...just page after page of spells and recipes and the occasional illustration of a warlock or vampire.

About halfway through, Lux found something. "A Magical Suction Spelle," he read.

PULLETH THE MAGIC FROM OUT A CYRSE AS PULLING POISONE FROM THE BYTE OF A SNAYKE.

"That sounds good."

At the top of the page, some long ago person wrote,

"Most Effective"

More exciting still, the spell required it be performed inside the bounds of a magic circle. "Yes." He jumped up. "Ritual magic! This is it!"

As fast as he could, Lux copied down the short list of ingredients. "Perfect! I've got all this stuff in my room, except the dittany and Mom has tons of that in the store." He also copied down the word of power, Expurgo, and stuck the whole list in his pocket.

With great care, Lux laid the old book on the mantle. Then he looked at the pile on the bed and sighed. "I can't take them. They're too heavy and it's probably not smart to have them in the house anyway. Not with Inquisitors snooping around." He walked to the door, promising himself he'd come back for the books as soon as he could.

Lux double-checked his list then locked up and slid the key back under the mat. At the top of the stairs, he found the portal open, just as he left it.

He concentrated on the closing notes. He chanted them slow and long. The tones rang against the old stones. A damp chill washed over him as the energy flowed back into the portal and he found himself in his regular basement.

I did it. I opened it and I closed it with no mistakes. Not one.

Smiling, he climbed the stairs to the store, wishing he could tell someone. *Mom and Dad would have a fit, but maybe I can tell Umbra. She'll understand.*

At the top of the stairs, he headed across the dark shop toward the jars of herbs. He filled a plastic bag with the dittany he needed. The clock over the counter said 4:30 am. He rubbed his eyes. *No wonder I'm wiped out. I was down there all night.*

The amber glow of streetlights filled the front of the store. Against the glare, Lux saw dark shapes milling around outside the windows. He drew back behind the herb shelves and peeked around.

Inquisitors!

In dark suits and hoods, five of them stood in front of the shop, like they were guarding the door. Lux crept from shadow to shadow until he reached the store room, then he ran upstairs. The hiccups started halfway up.

He raced into his parent's bedroom and pounced onto the bed. "Dad. Hic-Dad!"

"Lux?" said his father. "What is it? Are you sick?"

"Inquisitors," Lux whispered. "In front of the store. Five. Five!"

Cerri bolted upright. Atlas jumped out of bed and peeked through the curtains. His voice grim, he said, "Five at least. Probably more at the back door."

"I don't suppose they're here to keep people from getting in," Cerri said. "What do we do?"

Atlas pulled on a robe. "We need to get out of here. Cerri, get Umbra up. Lux, did you pack your bag last night for Aunt Sophia's house?"

"Yes," said Lux.

His mother hurried down the hall into Umbra's room.

"Go get it," said Atlas. "Get Umbra's too. Take them both down to the kitchen. But quietly. And no lights!"

As Lux rushed down the hall, his mother explained what was happening to Umbra. *That's a nice way to wake up. Rise and shine, dear. Inquisitors are breaking in.*

Umbra's bag sat in front of her door. Lux picked it up then ducked into his room to get his.

In the light from the window, Lux saw his herb jars glittering in the corner. He paused a second, then grabbed his school backpack and swept them all into it. *If we're going to Aunt Sophia's, I'll have plenty of time to work the spell there.*

Zipping the pack shut, he pulled it over his shoulder. He took the two suitcases and headed downstairs to wait in the dark kitchen for the rest of his family. A few minutes later, the door swung open, but no one came in.

"Umbra?" he asked.

Her footsteps crossed the room, and she sat down next to Lux.

"Are you scared?" he asked.

She squeezed once.

"Me too," he said.

They waited an eternity until Cerri came through the door.

"...can't take the car. Even if they let us leave, they'd probably follow us."

"You'll have to come down with me," said Atlas. "And we better hurry, before they decide to come in."

"Let's get going, kids," she said. "Lux, Umbra, do you have your shoes on?"

Lux's heart raced as he tied his shoes. *Not taking the car? Aunt Sophia's house is six miles from the edge of town. We can't walk that...not with suitcases and Inquisitors hanging around. And there's only one other way to get there: Ley Lines.*

Chapter Eleven

"Dad!" whispered Lux. "Are we taking the you-know-what?"

"What you-know-what?"

Lux pointed to the floor. "The ley lines."

Atlas sighed. "Yes, we're taking the ley network. Now come on! Those Inquisitors could come in any minute." He turned back to Cerri and murmured instructions.

Lux picked up his suitcase and watched as Umbra's rubber boots shaped like bumblebees disappeared one at a time as she put them on. *The ley network! We're actually going on the ley lines. This almost makes up for missing the Gathering.*

"Let's go," said Atlas.

Lux jumped up. "Do you want me to carry anything?"

"We've got the luggage," said his father. "I just want you to keep track of your sister. Once you're in the ley terminal, make sure no one notices her. That means, no one trips over her, sits on her, bumps into her or anything else. Just because you're going to be around other wiccaes doesn't mean her invisibility will be accepted any better." Atlas opened the door to the stairs. "Hurry!"

Cerri walked out, followed by Lux and Umbra. Atlas closed and locked the door. Lux felt a sudden clutch in his stomach. *How long will we be gone? The last time Dad went on this kind of trip, he didn't come home for weeks. What if…*

Lux rubbed his forehead. *Shut up! The Gathering is just a meeting. A meeting isn't scary.*

The four of them crept down the stairs. Lux peeked around the edge of the storeroom door. The Inquisitors still lurked in front of the store. *And Dad said there's more outside the back door.* Lux half expected it to burst open as they crept by. Before they reached the basement, his hiccups started again.

His mother opened the portal this time. Lux leaned close to listen to the tones, almost humming them himself. He so lost himself in the notes that when the energy ripple flowed out, he fell into a heap on the stone floor. Umbra giggled. Atlas put one large hand under Lux's arm and lifted him to his feet.

"Well, if no one felt the energy shift, I'm sure they felt the tremors from that fall!" he said. "Not to mention the hiccups."

"Sorry," mumbled Lux. He grabbed Umbra's hand and followed Cerri through the arch. "Have you been down here before?" he asked Umbra.

Two squeezes…no.

110

Good. That makes up for her knowing about the second basement before I did.

Atlas closed the portal behind them as Cerri started down the stone steps. The torches still burned and the large room at the bottom stood empty as ever. They continued past the ley-over. As they neared the end of the corridor, Lux saw a wide flight of steps going down. From the top, it looked endless. Three flights, with landings between, stretched through the dim light. He couldn't even see the bottom. On the second landing an electric lamp lit an old-fashioned tin sign that read, "The Ramsbottom".

With enough room to walk four abreast, they started down the stairs together.

"Dad," said Lux. "Is that the pub where Crowley was?"

"Yes. The Ramsbottom." Atlas smiled. "No better place on Earth."

Cerri chuckled.

"Really?" Lux asked.

"Well—that's what the T-shirts say," said Atlas. "It's sort of a joke, because they aren't really on our Earth, you know."

"We're on a different planet?"

"No." Atlas sighed. "We have so much work to do! When this little episode is over, you kids are going to have magic training every day. We should never have waited. Ridiculous law."

Lux tried to take his mind off the Inquisitors by thinking about what spells and skills he might do. *I'll do levitation first. Then, I'll try some of those potions in the poisonous herb book from the ley-over. After that...*

An enormous archway marked the end of the stairway; that, and quite a bit of noise. They passed through the opening, carved with some sort of Egyptian-looking flowers, and entered a cavernous vaulted room.

Huge chunks of polished black and white marble formed the floor. The walls seemed to be solid rock, carved in the same Egyptian style as the archway. The vaulted ceiling contained thousands of tiny carved squares, and high in the center ran an enormous cylinder of rough black rock. On either side of it, tall metal arms reached up and over the cylinder, suspending it above the floor. Skeletal iron stairs clung to the arms, supporting small catwalks on either side of the cylinder.

That's gotta be the ley line.

Lit only with torches, shadows filled the tunnel. So did people. Wiccaes of every make and model rushed by. In one direction, the black cylinder continued through the vaulted room and disappeared into a flat face of solid rock. In the other direction, Lux could see that several tunnels converged. Two other black ley line cylinders crossed beneath the first at awkward angles.

Atlas began walking in that direction. Cerri nudged Lux to follow him. He led Umbra by the arm, holding her very close. He remembered his father's instructions about not letting anyone notice her. She squeezed his hand tight and didn't let go. *Umbra's nervous.*

At the convergence, the ceiling soared higher. Not just three, but seven black ley lines crossed through the room. Small ticket windows lined the walls and people stood before them. Above the windows signs listed destinations: London, Mykonos, Angkor Wat. His parents sat their luggage down on a stone bench and rested.

"Mom," he asked. "Can you really get to London from here?"

"Yes. You can get just about anywhere from here," she answered. "Sometime soon we should take a trip together. Wouldn't that be nice?" She turned to Atlas. "Just like the old days."

Altas frowned. "It would be nice. It would be nicer if there weren't Inquisitors outside the store. I'm afraid the 'old days' we're going to get won't be the happy ones."

Wow. We're breaking the law. All four of us, or...well, all gazillion of us. People filled the terminal, and none of them seemed too concerned about using an illegal ley network.

"What happens if we get caught down here?" Lux tried to sound nonchalant.

"We won't, Lux," assured his father. "Remember, Sprenger refuses to use magic, which means he has no way to access these tunnels. While we're in the terminal, we're perfectly safe. It's going

113

in or out through known portals that is potentially dangerous."

"Does that mean they could be waiting for us outside the portal in our basement? Or outside wherever we're going now?" He wrinkled his forehead. "Where exactly are we going now?"

"Quiet," said his father. "I said known portals. Neither of the portals you'll use today are known to anyone outside the family. And we need to keep it that way. You'll be at your aunt's house in about an hour."

His mom smiled. "Everything will be fine, Lux. I promise."

Lux breathed easier. Umbra loosened her death grip on his hand and circulation returned to his little finger. A loud rattle sounded overhead. A steel cable with a huge magnetic disc attached to the end swung down through a cleft in the ceiling. It zoomed along, running right above the ley line, and two similar cables appeared behind it. Next came a series of heavy thuds and then, with a sonic 'whoosh' and a metallic clap, three silver train cars emerged from the top of the ley line and attached themselves to the hanging cables. Loud squealing indicated some sort of brakes. As Lux watched, the cars slowed and stopped just short of the rock wall at the far end of the terminal.

"They cut that kind of close, didn't they?" his mother said.

"Wow! That was so cool!" Lux cried. "Is that our train? How do we get on? Shouldn't we get our tickets? Wow! Wait 'til I tell Cyril about this!"

"I'm glad you're impressed, Lux," his father said. "But I'm afraid you can't tell Cyril. This must be kept completely secret, remember?"

Lux nodded. "All right. Cyril's not speaking to me anyway."

"That is not your train. In fact, it's not a train at all. The ley vehicles are called coaches. You'll be taking Aunt Sophia's private coach, which is not as modern nor as large at that one. But it does have a certain coolness." Atlas smiled. "We better get moving. You should be leaving in twenty minutes. And I need to get my coach to Toledo if I'm going to attend The Gathering." He headed through the ticket area and turned down a much smaller corridor marked "Private Coach Boarding."

Sconces lit the arched ceiling of the hallway, illuminating frescos of different magical legends. Whitewash brightened the walls. A thick Persian rug covered the floor and muffled their steps. The long corridor sloped toward a door at the end marked "Private Coach Passengers Only". As they approached it, Atlas took a key ring out of this coat pocket. He fit a shiny key into the brass lock and turned it three times around. *Just like the ley-over.*

Lux heard a tiny click and the door swung open to reveal a circular room filled with expensive furniture.

Atlas dropped his bags. "This is odd. Why aren't there any people in here?"

"Good question," said a man's voice. The door banged shut.

They turned to find three huge guys wearing black uniforms embroidered with two Gothic "M"s on the chest. *Murklin's Murderers!* Worse, walking toward them from the far side of the room strode an all-too-familiar figure wearing a fur hat with a gold medallion.

"Murklin." Lux stepped in front of Umbra just as his mother pushed them both behind her. Atlas strode toward Murklin.

"Atlas," said Murklin. "My friend, it's been too long."

"How did you get in here, Ambrose? A bit deep for your diggers, isn't it?"

Murklin's white eyes rolled. "I have no compunction against using magic. You are confusing me with Mr. Sprenger. I simply popped down here from the Elm Street portal. You remember the Elm Street portal, don't you? We spent a great deal of time there in our days at Falmer. Ah, memories..." He turned to Lux. "Did you know your father and I went to boarding school together? So you see, we're old friends. In fact, why don't you call me Uncle Ambrose?"

He crossed to Cerri and held out his hand. "Where are my manners? How very nice to see you again, Mrs. St. Clare. Always a pleasure."

Cerri shrank away from him.

"No?" he asked. "You prefer not to shake my hand? Very well then, perhaps the young master would be more accommodating."

Murklin grabbed Cerri by the arm and yanked her aside.

"No!" Lux shouted. "Mom!"

Atlas lunged to catch her, but she hit the floor hard. Guards appeared on either side of Atlas. They grabbed his arms and wrestled him away from Cerri. Lux looked on with horror, and didn't even notice that Umbra had wriggled out of his grasp.

"What do you want with us?" Atlas demanded.

"I have a very special opportunity for you," he said. "Now then, young man." He extended his hand to Lux. "Just put your hand out. It's quite simple."

"No," said Lux. "I'd rather shake hands with a snake."

Murklin grabbed Lux's hand and twisted his arm behind his back.

"Ow!" Lux cried.

"There we go," said Murklin. "Now, was that so bad?"

Lux's backpack swung on his shoulder, but Murklin held him tight. That's when it dawned on him.

Umbra! She's gone.

He looked up at Murklin. Whatever happened, Lux needed to keep him from finding Umbra.

"I said, 'was that so bad?'" Murklin squeezed his fingers together.

Lux grimaced and glared into Murklin's blank eyes. "Yeah, actually. It was."

"Like your mother, you have no manners," he said. "Lovely. If I need to kill you it will be that much easier." Murklin turned to his men. "We're wasting time. Take Mr. and Mrs. St. Clare out to the boarding area. But...wait." He looked around. "One, two, three... Only three. There should be another. The girl." He spun Lux around, wrapping his hand around his neck. "Where is your sister?"

"Ch...chicken pox," choked Lux.

"Chicken...what?"

"Chicken pox," Lux repeated. "It's a disease where you get--"

"I know what chicken pox are!" said Murklin. "What does that have to do with your sister?"

"She has chicken pox," Lux pushed Murklin's hand off his neck. "She's at my Aunt's house--"

"Lux!" yelled Atlas. "That's enough."

Murklin smiled. "So the wee St. Clare is out at Six Mile Farm, is she? Well, we can deal with small potatoes later. Let's move."

Atlas glared over his shoulder at Murklin as the guards dragged him through a door. Murklin

118

pushed Lux after his mother then paused. He turned back, as if to make sure no one stayed behind.

Lux's heart hammered in his chest. *Why's he stopping? Can he see Umbra?* For a split second, Lux felt certain he did. Thinking quick, he brought his heel backward as hard as he could, kicking Murklin in the shin.

"Ow!" Murklin shoved Lux, who fell through the door and onto the pavement outside. Lux jumped up just as Murklin came through the door himself. The man wrapped his arm around Lux's neck. Despite the choking, Lux smiled. Murklin hadn't found Umbra.

Now she can get out into the terminal and find someone to help us. 'Course it'll have to be someone who'll trust a six-year old. And who won't be freaked out because she's invisible. And who'll understand her even though she can't speak. Lux groaned. *We're doomed.*

Murklin dragged him across a large parking lot. A hundred or so ley coaches sat in neat rows, some long, some short, some dented, some new. Five coaches sat apart from the rest, lined up front to back, prepped and ready to fly.

That second one's gotta be Aunt Sophia's. The varnished wood gleamed and gold filigreed letters across the back spelled "Icarus". *It's the nicest one here, even though it's old.*

"Now then," said Murklin. "Shall we get started?"

"What are you doing, Ambrose?" demanded Atlas. "If it's me you want, let my family go. There's no reason to involve them."

"I'm afraid there is every reason to involve them," said Murklin. "We're interested in all of you. Or rather, a certain part of each of you."

He reached into his coat and pulled out what looked like an old railroad spike. It was black metal, about seven inches long and shaped like a "T". The top arms curled upward in little spirals and the bottom ended in a sharp point.

"To be precise, I intend to take the magical part of you. I doubt it will hurt...much, though I can't say for sure. But once it's over, you're all free to go...dead or alive." He smiled. "Shall we get started? Who wants to go first?"

Chapter Twelve

"Great Gods!" murmured Atlas. "The Iron Bodkin."

No way! Lux craned his neck to get a better look. *A Tool of Legend...right in front of me!* "So it actually does exist?"

Murklin rolled his eyes. "Obviously, since I'm holding it in my hand. Now, I'll ask again. Which of you wants the honor of being the first modern victim of this legendary witch-pricker?"

"Ambrose, what are you trying to accomplish with this?" said Atlas. "You know the St. Clare gift skipped me and Lux hasn't even been gifted yet. This seems like a lot of effort to take Cerri's clairvoyance."

"For one thing, the Ordinaricans want you out of the way," he said. "Second, we want to make sure this thing works. But most importantly, I'm sure you're aware of the legislation just passed regarding the registration of all children born to a magical parent."

Atlas raised one eyebrow. "Yes. What's your point?"

"My point?" Murklin looked at the sharp end of the spike. "It's actually the point of this wonderful tool which will make the strongest statement. And the statement we want to make is, No More Magic."

Lux understood first. "No way! You're going to stab all the Wiccae kids and take their magic? That's crap!"

"Impressive," said Murklin. "Not nearly as dense as your parents, are you?"

Atlas shook his head. "That would be hundreds of thousands of children every year! There aren't enough hours to perform that task! It's simply impossible."

Murklin nodded. "Yes, at first we'll probably only manage to inoculate half of the eligible children."

"Inoculate?" Cerri cried. "Is that what you're calling it? As if magic is a disease?"

Murklin ignored Cerri's outburst. "But by cutting the magical population, the next generation will be only half as large. In twenty years or so, we'll be able to completely rid all future generations of the plague which has terrorized us for so long."

Atlas laughed. "You, Ambo? Calling magic a 'plague'? Do you remember who you are?"

Murklin stiffened.

Atlas turned to the soldiers. "This man possesses so many magical gifts there was considerable speculation at school that he was one of the Two."

"Hang on," said Lux. He twisted around to see Murklin. "You're Wiccaen? Why are you doing this?"

Murklin pulled up on Lux's arm and spun him back around. "I hardly need to share my motivations with you."

"Is Sprenger blackmailing you?" Atlas asked. "Offering you money? Power? Tell me the truth!"

Murklin stared at Atlas for a moment. "The truth? Fine. The truth is, once this is over, you'll all be dead," said Murklin. "Is that enough truth for one day?"

Lux felt the blood drain from his face. *Dead?*

"Enough reminiscing!" cried Murklin. "I have tickets for the ballet tonight, and if I'm late my daughter will never forgive me." He motioned one of the guards over and handed Lux to him. "This young man will be our first volunteer." The guard threw Lux's backpack on the ground and gripped his arms.

"Excellent." Murklin stepped back, took a deep breath and chanted in a language Lux didn't understand.

Behind him, he heard his father and mother murmuring too. *They're trying to cast protection spells.* He sagged against the guard. *As if there's a spell that'll keep that spike from going right through me.* Lux struggled to look at his parents one last time, but the guard held him tight. *I don't want to die!*

123

Murklin stepped forward and pointed the bodkin right at Lux's chest. He pulled his arm back. "Expurgo!" he shouted. Then he thrust the tool forward.

His mother screamed. The bodkin slammed into Lux's chest. It knocked his breath away, but it didn't hurt like he thought it would. In fact, it didn't hurt at all. Lux opened his eyes. A yellow rubber boot, shaped like a bumblebee, covered Murklin's arm.

Murklin's jaw dropped. He pulled his arm back for a closer look but the boot shot off of his hand, taking the bodkin with it. Boot and bodkin both landed with a clatter several feet away. Murklin lunged for the bodkin. His fingers stretched toward the Tool of Legend, almost reaching the handle.

But it disappeared!

"Where did it go?" His scream echoed through the empty parking lot. "Find it! Don't just stand there! I must have that bodkin!"

The guards holding Atlas and Cerri let them go and raced in circles, bumping into each other.

"Where is it?" Murklin screamed.

Lux smiled. *Umbra's got the bodkin.*

He ran to his parents. Cerri grabbed him and started toward the door. Lux felt around. *Where is Umbra?*

They reached the door to the ley terminal. Murklin picked up the bumblebee boot and turned to them.

"I have seen this before!" he said. "Upstairs in that god-forsaken rat hole you people call a home! It's too small for any of your feet! Where is she?" He grabbed Atlas by his tie. "Where is the girl?"

Atlas didn't answer.

Murklin pushed Atlas away and turned to Lux. "Where is your sister?"

"Stop it!" yelled Cerri. "Leave him alone."

"I don't know," Lux replied. "And I wouldn't tell you if I did."

Murklin grasped a handful of Lux's hair and pulled him away from his parents. Atlas rushed forward. Guards surrounded him and forced him to the ground.

Murklin jerked Lux's hair. "Where is she?"

"I'm not telling you anything!" Lux screamed.

"Fine," said Murklin. "You're going into the ley tunnel."

For one brief moment, Lux thought Murklin planned to put him in a coach and send him away. The thought died as Murklin dragged him, not toward the coaches, but toward the dark, sloping tunnel across the tarmac.

Lux struggled and pushed as the man pulled him toward the gaping entrance. As they drew near the tunnel, Lux heard another sound beneath his parents' screams.

A low hum, almost a vibration, came from the ground. The closer they got to the ley tunnel, the more the sound grew.

Murklin paused. He heard it too. Then a distant clatter came from inside the tunnel.

Murklin grinned and his scarred, red eyelid crinkled up. "Aren't you lucky!" he said. "I hoped you would last a few agonizing hours bathing in ley energy. But alas, no lingering death for you! Your fate lies on the fender of that approaching coach." He laughed as he dragged Lux the last twenty yards to the corridor. "Be sure to write!"

Murklin flung him into the darkened tunnel. Cerri screamed.

Lux's feet flew out from under him on the slick ramp floor.

"No!" he cried.

The more Lux thrashed, the further down he slid. The coach scraped and clattered ahead, still some distance off. Lux flipped onto his back and grabbed at the walls of the tunnel. His hands met nothing but cold, smooth rock. He tried to turn sideways and wedge himself to a stop. His feet didn't reach the opposite wall.

The angle of the floor increased. Lux picked up speed. The coach banged into the stone walls as it approached. *It's going to crush me!*

"Hey! Stop! I'm here."

As he slid down the tunnel, the clattering came closer and closer. "Stop! Hey. Hey!"

"To the top," Spinnet's voice yelled in his head.

"Mr. Spinnet?"

"To the top, boy. The top!" yelled Spinnet even louder. Lux saw the headlight of the coach shining through the darkness. *I really don't want to die.*

"To the top," Spinnet cried.

"Where are you?" Lux yelled. "What does that mean?"

He cast his eyes toward the ceiling, now visible as the coach came nearer. Something whizzed by. Peering through the gloom, Lux glimpsed a lot of somethings whizzing by. He pushed into a sitting position and launched himself toward the ceiling, fingers outstretched. A metal rung brushed his fingertips.

"Handles!" Lux said.

"Yes, handles," replied Spinnet's voice. "Now get to the top!"

Lux lunged for the next few handles and managed to catch one. He dangled from the ceiling and stared at the headlight coming toward him.

"Now what?"

"Feet up," replied Spinnet's voice.

Lux struggled to pull his feet up and managed to brace them on the next handle. The tunnel sloped a lot at that point, so most of Lux's weight rested on his feet. Still, his arms ached.

What's going to keep me from sliding into the ley tunnel after the coach passes? I'll die just like Murklin wanted. How is this better?

"Mr Spinnet," he yelled into the darkness. "I don't think this is helping."

The coach crept along. With the headlight shining in his eyes, Lux couldn't make out much detail, but it didn't seem to be shaped like the other vehicles. *It looks more like a bulldozer. It even sounds like a bulldozer with that engine.* Lux's arms ached. The coach banged closer, just yards away now. The engine roared.

Engine? Lux strained to peer past the headlight. *Ley coaches don't have engines. They move by ley energy and magnets.* Lux heard the rumble of a motor and smelled acrid exhaust.

"Mr. Spinnet, where are you?"

The headlight passed beneath Lux and he glimpsed the vehicle. At the front stood a flat deck lined with tool boxes. *It's a repair car. I can drop onto it and ride out.*

"Yes," said Spinnet's voice. "Exactly! First and ten. Tally-ho!"

Lux let go of the rungs and landed with a thud. He rubbed his arms as he looked around.

"Hello?" he said. No one answered.

As the car plodded its steady course up the corridor, Lux considered what would happen once he reached the top. *Murklin will still be there, and Mom and Dad will still be hostages. What am I supposed to do then? Murklin will just toss me back into the tunnel.*

"Stand firm, dear boy. Help is on the way," said Spinnet.

Lux looked around. "Mr Spinnet?" he said. "Where are you?"

128

"I am where I am," he answered. "Aren't you where you are?"

"Um..." Lux peered around in the gloom, looking for the old man. "I guess so."

"Thank Heavens!" Spinnet said.

The end of the corridor came into view. "What am I supposed to do now?" he asked.

"Stand firm" was the answer.

In the gathering light, Lux saw that he stood on the metal deck of a large yellow train-like vehicle, above an engine that belched blue smoke. Behind the deck, a cab housed a steering mechanism and numerous gauges and dials. Through the windshield Lux spied a door that led to the rear of the vehicle. As he watched, the door opened and into the cab stepped--

"Crowley!" Lux's voice echoed through the corridor.

Crowley jerked to attention and spotted Lux on the deck. His jaw dropped.

"Lux?" His uncle reached around the windshield and hauled him into the cab. "What the heck are you doing? You could have died!"

Lux grinned with relief and threw his arms around Crowley. "Murklin threw me into the tunnel because I wouldn't tell him where Umbra was."

"Holy Hertha!" said Crowley. "Well, you're safe for the moment. Hold on to this bar. We're coming into the terminal and I need to start steering this thing." He grinned. "I've never driven a tunnel rat before. Spinnet told me how they work, but I think things have changed a lot since he drove one. This might be a really bumpy ride."

"I don't care about bumps," Lux replied. "But can't it go any faster? Mom and Dad are still up there with Murklin."

"It can go faster, but I've got about a hundred witches in the back I'm trying not to spill."

It was Lux's turn to drop his jaw. "You've got wiccaes? In the back of this?"

"Yep," Crowley replied. "By the time AnSo and Spinnet figured out what was going on, the covens had already begun to gather. When I left the serpent mounds, I had sixty people with me, and we picked up more on the way. Everyone wanted to help with the rescue." He looked through the windshield just as the terminal building came into view. "Murklin won't know what hit him."

Chapter Thirteen

Lux held his breath as the tunnel rat chugged onto the tarmac. The light of the loading area blinded him. He shielded his eyes with his arm and stared at his parents.

"Hey, something's wrong with Mom," Lux said. "She's crying!"

"Well," said Crowley. "She thinks you're dead, so yeah!"

"Oh right."

Everyone on the tarmac turned toward them as the vehicle emerged from the tunnel.

Lux waved at his mom and dad. "It's me! I'm ok!"

Murklin yelled to his guards. They ran toward the vehicle, crouched down and pulled out guns.

"They're going to shoot us!" yelled Lux.

"Nah." Crowley picked up a walkie talkie. "Protection spells, now!"

A low rumble vibrated through the air as the witches shouted, "Fendere!" Something warm flowed around Lux and then -- nothing.

"Did it work?" he asked.

Crowley laughed. "Lux, that spell was just cast by a hundred of the strongest witches in the United States. You've never been safer in your life. Watch."

One of the guards stood up and pointed his gun at them. Crowley smiled and waved as the guard pumped the trigger over and over. The bullets exploded in little sparkles as they hit the protection spell and disappeared.

"Whoa, cool!" said Lux.

"Seriously," agreed Crowley. "I've never seen them evaporate like that."

"You've been shot at before?" Lux asked.

Crowley picked up the walkie talkie again. "All right, folks. Protection spell is in place and successful. Get ready to hit the ground."

He slowed the tunnel rat to a stop. More guards surrounded them and fired their guns. Bullets sparkled all around them like fireworks.

"What now?" Lux asked.

Crowley smiled. "Just watch."

Murklin's guards continued to shoot as they backed away. The witches pushed the boundaries of the spell outward and gave themselves room to disembark. A swelling tide of black robed figures advanced on the guards.

132

One of the wiccaes shouted *Apium Transformo.*
The firing stopped as the guards' guns changed into
celery sticks. After a quiet moment, Murklin's
Murderers, every last scary one of them, turned and
ran.

Witches with black robes flying scurried here
and there. Some raised their hand and levitated a
fleeing guard or conjured ropes from thin air. Most of
Murklin's men fled through the parking lot; others
tried to get into the terminal. Still others made the
poor choice of running into the corridor leading to the
ley tunnel.

In the midst of it all, Murklin stalked toward
Lux's parents.

"Crowley! Look," Lux cried. "What's Murklin
doing?"

"He's going after Cerri and Atlas," Crowley
replied. He yanked on the emergency brake. "Stay
here, Lux. Don't leave the car." Crowley leapt off the
tunnel rat and sprinted across the parking lot toward
the terminal door, where Atlas and Cerri backed
away from Murklin.

"Murklin!" Crowley grabbed the only thing he
could find at the moment, which happened to be
Umbra's yellow boot, and hurled it toward the man.
Murklin turned just in time to catch the boot in the
face. He went down, holding his bloody nose.

Murklin shouted "Avolo!" Crowley soared
backward and landed hard on the tarmac.

Stay here? Lux fumed. *I'm sick of sitting on the sidelines. Besides, Crowley's not exactly saving the day.*

Lux jumped off the vehicle and raced toward his parents. He stopped behind the ley coaches to formulate a plan. Murklin strode toward Crowley, his hands raised in front of him. Lux picked up his backpack which lay on the tarmac a few feet ahead of him. He planned to swing it at Murklin and knock him down. But as he swung the pack forward, someone grabbed his arm. He turned with his fist in the air, but no one was there.

"Umbra!" he whispered. One squeeze. "Thank the gods!"

Several wiccaes rushed passed him and advanced on Murklin. They worked magic to restrain the man. But Atlas was right when he said Murklin had many magical gifts. As quickly as ropes bound the man's arms, they changed into wet noodles and fell apart. Giant nets fell from the ceiling, then turned into spider webs and blew away.

Lux took a step toward Murklin but Umbra grabbed him. "I have to help," he said.

She grabbed his hand and laid something in it. When she let go, a long black spike appeared in his hand.

As Lux stared at the bodkin, a plan crystalized in his head. "We don't have time to cast a circle," he said. "I hope it works without one."

He and Umbra dumped his jars of herbs onto the tarmac. Lux read off ingredients. "Pinch of

134

dittany, two knife blades of nightshade, eight drops essence of calendula."

Umbra opened vials and poured the different leaves and liquids into an empty jar. After the last ingredient, Lux drove the point of the spike into the mixture.

Holding the bodkin, he stood up and looked around for Murklin. The man battled a dozen wiccaes not far away. Two of the wiccaes fell to the ground clutching their heads. Murklin waved at three others and they disappeared. Three more turned and ran away. Murklin whirled around to face four more who conjured ropes around his wrists. Murklin held his arms out and the ropes shattered.

He won't beat this! At full speed, Lux raced toward the man. The heat of the spells flew around him. Staring at Murklin's back, he wondered...

Where do I stab him? In the chest? In the back? Will it make a difference? What if--what if it kills him?

Lux slowed a bit. *I don't want to kill anybody.*

"Not even Murklin?" asked a voice in his head.

Lux tripped over something lying on the tarmac and soared through the air with the bodkin tight in his hand. He closed his eyes just as he crashed into Murklin. The bodkin plunged into the man's flesh.

"Expurgo," cried Lux. The force of the spell blew him back. He landed hard and stars exploded in his eyes.

Murklin shrieked in pain. Lux tried to sit up, but his head spun.

"What have you done?" the man cried. He pulled the bodkin out of his thigh. The terminal grew quiet.

Very quiet.

Murklin stared at the bodkin in his hand and then at Lux. "What did you say?"

"Expurgo," Lux said. "I know that spell. It takes the magic out of a curse. Or out of a person."

Murklin sneered as he limped toward Lux. "You stupid, stupid boy," he said. "It takes more than magic words to cast that spell."

Lux scuttled away from him like a crab. "You're right. It takes calendula, bitterroot and a bunch of other stuff."

Murklin stopped. His face turned stark white. "Calendula...but..." He shook his head. "Where would you find calendula here? You're bluffing."

"Lux," Cerri cried. "Get away from him."

Lux didn't move. Instead he pointed to his backpack and the pile of herbs sitting next to it. "I brought my own."

Murklin's face changed to a frightening shade of red. "You have no idea what you've done!" He lunged toward Lux but tripped over the same thing Lux had tripped over. Murklin fell to the floor, a yellow bumblebee boot lying at his feet. Wiccaes sprang into action and imprisoned Murklin in a web of ropes.

136

"You've taken my powers!" he whispered. His white eyes narrowed at Lux. "You'll regret this. If it takes every waking hour of my life, I will have my revenge! You have no idea what you've done!"

Lux frowned and rubbed his head.

"Ha!" Crowley grinned. "How's it feel to be brought down by an eleven-year old?"

Cerri pulled Lux away and smothered him in a massive hug. Several other witches patted him on the back.

"That was very brave," said a woman with red hair.

"That's quite a boy you've got there, Cerri," an older lady told his mom.

"Ambrose," said Atlas. "You'll be in no position to avenge anything for a long, long time. You've broken so many laws today, I doubt you'll even have another 'waking hour' as a free man."

Murklin snorted. "Have you forgotten who runs the prisons? Mr. Sprenger is a dear friend of mine. I'll never even see the inside of a cell."

Atlas took the bodkin out of Murklin's roped hand. "I wasn't talking about Capitol Prison. I had in mind something a bit more family oriented." He turned to a woman standing nearby. "Madam Ramsbottom, do you still have those warlock stocks at your estate?"

"I do," she said. "They'd be pleased to have some visitors again!"

"You can't be serious," said Murklin. "You can't just lock me away in your own private dungeon. I have rights! Even under the Wiccaen Code of Ethics you can't do that."

"You forfeited your rights when you turned your back on the Craft. The Code of Ethics only applies to people who are willing to live by it," said Atlas. He looked sad. "Ambo, I never expected you would come to this."

Murklin stared back at him. "Atlas, you have no idea what you are about to do."

"I think I do," he said. "It's my job to make this country safe for the Wiccae. Putting you away will do that."

Murklin rolled his eyes.

Atlas motioned for the Ramsbottom lady. She stepped forward with two other men who grasped Murklin by the arms.

"We'll take him right away," she said. "I'll be in touch tomorrow." Atlas nodded. She gave Cerri a hug before she turned to Lux. "You should be very proud of yourself, Lux. You showed true courage, and that's a rare gift."

Lux blushed. "Thanks."

Ms. Rambsbottom joined the men holding Murklin. Together, the three witches raised their arms a little and all four disappeared.

Cerri called for Umbra. Lux picked up her yellow boot and called too. Before long, he felt a tug on his shirt and Umbra's small hand grasped his own.

"Here she is, Mom." Lux gave his invisible sister a hug and handed her back her boot. It disappeared as soon as he let go of it.

She giggled as Cerri grabbed her and sobbed with relief. Some of the witches standing nearby began whispering. Lux remembered Atlas saying that Umbra's invisibility would not be tolerated any better by witches than by regular folks.

"It's my fault she's invisible," Lux said. "I was mixing a potion to make peas taste like strawberries and I guess something went wrong." Lux hung his head. The whispering witches chuckled.

A couple wiccaes offered suggestions on how to reverse the potion. Cerri nodded and thanked each of them, not bothering to say they had already tried them.

Lux grinned. *I stopped Murklin. Me. Without any mistakes! And with a little help from Mr. Spinnet.* Lux scanned the crowd, but he didn't see Spinnet.

"Crowley," he called. "Did Mr. Spinnet already leave?"

"Spinnet wasn't here," said his uncle.

"Yes he was," Lux said. "He was yelling at me in the tunnel. He told me how to get on the tunnel rat."

Crowley raised one eyebrow. "You heard Spinnet's voice in the tunnel?"

"Yeah. He told me about the handles on the ceiling, and to…to stand firm. I'm sure it was him.

The things he said didn't make any sense; only Spinnet talks like that."

Crowley laughed. "I know what you mean. But, seriously Lux, he wasn't here. We left him at the serpent mounds with Aunt Sophia. They were going to the farm to work some more spells. Dude, I don't know what you heard, but it wasn't Spinnet."

"Yes, it was," said Lux. "I know it was."

His father rubbed his chin. "Lux, you're certain the voice you heard belonged to Leeward Spinnet?"

Lux looked him square in the eye. "I'm positive."

"And where was the voice coming from?" he asked.

"Well, it was sort of…above me, or maybe in front of me. I'm not sure," Lux answered. "Things echo in that tunnel."

Cerri whispered something to Atlas.

"I'm not sure if anything is impossible anymore," his father said. "Lux, can you talk to Mr. Spinnet now?"

"Uh…no," said Lux. "He's not here."

"We'll have to sort this out later," Atlas said. "Right now, we need to get these people back to their homes for lunch."

Lux yawned and stretched his arms. *No wonder I'm tired. It's almost noon and I didn't sleep at all last night.*

"Leave it to me, Atlas." Crowley walked toward the tunnel rat, calling, "Anybody here want a lift home?"

Many voices called "No!" The remaining wiccaes made their way in every direction except toward the tunnel rat.

"Hey! C'mon," said Crowley. "My driving wasn't that bad--was it?"

Atlas patted his shoulder. "I'm sure your driving was fine, Crowley. But what do you say we take Icarus, just for kicks?" He motioned toward Aunt Sophia's gleaming coach.

"Well..." Crowley said. "I guess it would be faster."

Cerri smiled. "Great! But just to clarify, little brother, you're not driving."

Lux heaved a sigh of relief as they headed toward Aunt Sophia's coach.

Murklin can't bother us anymore and even though Umbra's still invisible, at least we're all safe. Plus, we're going to Aunt Sophia's house and she's bound to have some crazy huge meal for us. Maybe even pie!

Chapter Fourteen

Atlas opened the door to Icarus. Lux sprinted in, excited to see the inside. He found a small living room with two leather arm chairs and a chintz sofa. Behind the sofa stood a bar and mini refrigerator stocked with drinks. Lux and Umbra took all the crackers and cookies from the cabinets and piled them on the floor next to their sodas.

"I'm starving." Lux shoved two cookies into his mouth.

Atlas made himself a drink then climbed into the front of the coach. Lux grabbed a handful of crackers and followed his dad into the driver's chambers. His eyes widened. *Whoa. This is so different from a car.*

Instead of a steering wheel, the ley coach contained a telephone and a tiny blank computer screen. Atlas picked up the phone and dialed three numbers.

"Good evening, ley control. This is Atlas St. Clare. I'm afraid we were detained and are late getting off. Would it be possible to get Icarus into the queue?" He waited, then said, "Just out to Six-Mile Farm, heading north on the Glasgow line." Another pause. "Wonderful. Thank you very much." He hung up the phone and looked over his shoulder at Lux. "Come here."

Lux edged into the co-pilot's seat and sat down.

"I am so proud of you," Atlas said. "Not just for stopping Murklin, though that was very brave and showed quick thinking. I'm more impressed with the way you've handled the past week or so. I know this must have been a really difficult time for you, with Umbra's invisibility, and Cerri and Aunt Sophia being so busy with everything. Your mother said you haven't complained once. You're really growing up."

Lux felt his face heat up. "Well," he said, "it wouldn't have helped to complain. Not really." He remembered how much he wanted to unload his Cyril troubles on Atlas the other day. He smiled, glad he hadn't gotten the chance. "So, how does this thing work?"

"The coaches are moved along by the power of our own intention," said Atlas. "And they travel along paths of particle matter that serve as a conduit for our intention. Those paths are the ley lines."

"So, a ley line is kinda like a highway," said Lux. "Cars...I mean, coaches can go in either direction?"

"Yes. And everything goes at the same speed," his dad said.

"But how do they get in? Do they just slide down the tunnel like I did?"

"The coaches are pulled into the ley line with a large magnet."

"And once they're in," said Lux, "the ley energy moves them along. What happens at the other end? A big magnet pulls you out?"

"Exactly," said Atlas. He looked at the computer screen which blinked a diagram of their journey. "Except that the ley energy doesn't really 'move' us. We move ourselves using the ley energy. That's how traffic can run both ways in one tunnel. By using the intention jets..." Atlas launched into an explanation of intention jets. Lux fell asleep.

The next thing Lux knew, he was waking up in a soft feather bed at Aunt Sophia's house. *Whoa. What happened to the rest of yesterday? I don't even remember leaving the ley coach.*

Sunlight streamed through the dusty window and Lux smelled breakfast. He leapt out of bed, threw open the door and looked down a long arched hallway with uneven wood floors. He smiled. *I have never been in this room, I've never seen this hallway and I don't think I've seen a wood floor at Aunt Sophia's, ever.* "I love this house!"

He raced back into the room and pulled on his clothes. Digging a pencil out of his school bag, he headed back to the hall. After drawing a small arrow on the wall, he walked in that direction. *Even if I can't find the kitchen, at least, I'll be able to find my way back to my room. That time I got lost when I was seven, I just about starved.*

At the end of the hall, Lux found himself in the familiar round room his aunt called the Rotunda. Along the walls hung portraits of the Pickingill ancestors, which Aunt Sophia quizzed him on periodically.

Ok, the Rotunda I remember. The stairs...definitely not. He made his way down the white marble steps that wound around the edge of the room. *I don't even think there was a second floor last year, but if the kitchen is still in the same place, it should be right over...*

He pushed open a wood door to see a breakfast table groaning under the weight of a true Six-Mile-Farm feast. Lux's mouth watered.

Sausages and bacon filled one platter, a frittata with vegetables and cheese filled another. Belgian waffles sat next to a jug of warm maple syrup. Pitchers of orange juice and milk, coffee and tea, scattered around the table. Fresh fruit, biscuits, toast, danishes...

His family had already gathered around the old wooden table.

"Hello, sleeping head!" cried Spinnet. The old man sported a pink pillbox hat and a ratty blue terry cloth robe embroidered with a large red "Q".

Lux winced at the sight, but even Spinnet's revolting outfit didn't curb his appetite. He headed for an empty chair and plopped down...for a moment.

"Ah!" cried Umbra.

Lux jumped up. Everyone at the table burst into laughter.

"Are you ok?" Lux asked.

Umbra just giggled. Lux took a chair on the other side of the table.

"Nine point five for artistic impression," said Spinnet. "But just a three for technical marks."

Cerri sighed and looked at Atlas. "I wish there was something we could do about Umbra's invisibility. I hate the thought of her cooped up in the house all the time."

Atlas shrugged. "The only other option is to call a witch doctor and if we do that, the whole thing will be reported to the Magical Affairs Corps. That's the last thing we want."

Spinnet reached over and patted Umbra's hand. "Dear cherub," he said. "I think recess is over."

Crowley rolled his eyes.

Spinnet held his hand out toward Umbra. As everyone watched, a small bundle appeared in his hand. Right away, he dropped it on the table. Lux reached over to pick it up but Spinnet cried, "No dogs allowed!"

"Does that mean I'm not supposed to touch it?" Lux asked.

Spinnet turned to Umbra. "Skip the previews, dear girl, and let's have the feature presentation."

No one made a sound.

Is this crazy Spinnet talk, or is something really going to happen?

Aunt Sophia craned her neck over Spinnet's shoulder trying to get a look at the little bundle. Then, very slowly, Lux began to see a form sitting in Umbra's chair.

"That's it, dear," encouraged Spinnet. "First down. Ten yards to go."

Umbra became clearer and more solid. Her golden curls became distinct and her cheeks grew pink. She grinned as her hands became visible. No one moved until she seemed quite complete and Spinnet yelled, "Touchdown!"

Atlas whisked Umbra into a big hug. Cerri wrapped her arms around both of them.

Spinnet smiled and nodded. "And the extra point, too".

It's so weird to actually see Umbra again. Lux couldn't help but smile each time she looked at him.

Aunt Sophia used a spoon to nudge the little bundle onto a saucer and held it under her nose to inspect it. Leeward watched her. "No dogs allowed, dear" he warned.

She raised one eyebrow. "Are you behind this, Leeward?"

"Behind? No. In the middle, I am." He sipped his coffee. "Always in the middle."

"Behind what?" Cerri walked over to her aunt. Sophia handed the saucer to Cerri. She scrutinized what appeared to be a dried up old walnut. "For Brighid's sake, Leeward!" she exclaimed. "Did you give this to Umbra?"

"Yes. As I said, I came in the middle."

"What is it, Mom?" Lux asked.

Crowley took the saucer from Cerri and poked it himself.

"No dogs allowed!" repeated Spinnet.

Crowley frowned, but stopped poking.

"Why on earth would you do that?" Cerri cried.

"Mom, what is that thing?" Lux asked again.

"The cherub asked, and with good reason! Knew they were coming, she did. Nasty carpet baggers, stealing magic from good folks." He shook his head.

"What is he saying?" Cerri demanded.

"What is that thing?" Lux asked Crowley, who poked it again.

"Leeward, are you saying Umbra spoke to you?" asked Aunt Sophia.

"No Dogs Allowed!" thundered Spinnet, glaring at Crowley.

Aunt Sophia snatched the saucer away from Crowley and put it down in front of Spinnet. "Leeward," she said. "Look at me."

He stared her straight in the eye without flinching.

Impressive. Not many people can do that.

"Why did you give Umbra that charm?" She pointed to the little bundle.

"Because the cherub asked for it," he said.

"You're saying Umbra spoke to you?"

"Not in so many words." He smiled at Umbra. "She's very quiet, that one. Have you noticed that as well? Never says a word...."

"Leeward," Aunt Sophia said. "If Umbra did not speak to you using words, how did she speak to you?"

"Teletronically," he answered. "In my head, you know. Asked me to make her invisible because the traitor was coming with the spike."

Spinnet slurped his coffee, the only sound at the table. Lux looked at his sister. She stared at her plate.

Teletronically? Umbra spoke inside Spinnet's head? Hang on...

"Hey, Mr. Spinnet, did you talk to me in my head... teletronically... in the ley tunnel?"

"Yes, and I didn't appreciate your yelling. My hair is still ringing." He rubbed his pillbox hat.

"Telepathically," shouted Crowley. "He means telepathically, not 'teletronically'."

149

Atlas rolled his eyes. "Welcome to the group, Crowley. Did it really take you that long to figure it out?" He ducked as Crowley threw a biscuit at him.

"Stop that!" snapped Aunt Sophia. She turned back to Spinnet. "Yes, Leeward, I think the word you mean is telepathically. But I don't understand how Umbra knew Murklin was coming with the spike, which I assume means the bodkin. Her invisibility came before she issued her foretelling. How did she know any of those things before the foretelling?"

"How should I know?" Spinnet snapped. He pointed to Umbra. "Ask her!"

"I can't ask her, Leeward," was her patient reply. "She doesn't speak, and I can't communicate with her telepathically."

"Fine then. Ask him." He pointed this time to Lux. "He can do it. He's a teletronical speaker."

Lux's eyes widened. "I am?" He looked at Umbra. "Maybe I am. I could hear Spinnet in the tunnel. Maybe I can hear Umbra too."

"Umbra, dear," said Aunt Sophia. "Say something to your brother, telepathically."

"Teletronically!" Spinnet slapped the table.

Lux looked at Umbra. Her eyes wandered around the room for a moment then focused on Lux.

'How come the rooms are always different here?' said a voice in his head.

Lux grinned. "I don't know," he answered out loud. "I can't figure it out either."

150

"Lux?" Cerri bounced out of her chair. "Did you hear her? What did she say?"

"She wants to know why the rooms are always different here."

Cerri squealed. Aunt Sophia said to Umbra, "One day soon we'll explain that to you."

Lux laughed.

"What's so funny?" Crowley asked.

"I'm just happy I'm not the only one who gets told that!" he replied.

"Touché," said his father.

'We'll figure out the rooms ourselves,' Umbra said in his head.

Lux nodded. 'After breakfast.'

Cerri watched the silent exchange and groaned. "I'm not sure this telepathic communication is a good thing. They're already plotting something."

"They've been plotting things long before this," Aunt Sophia assured her.

Crowley sat down next to Umbra and whispered something in her ear.

'Crowley doesn't believe you can hear me,' she said.

Lux looked at his uncle. "I can hear her."

Crowley raised his eyebrows then whispered something else to Umbra. She wrinkled her nose but he motioned toward Lux.

'Crowley says for breakfast he had three scrambled eggs, four pieces of toast, a half pound of bacon, a bowl of cereal and a ham sandwich on rye.'

"Ugh. Really?" said Lux.

Umbra shrugged.

Lux looked at Crowley. "You ate eggs, toast, bacon, cereal and a sandwich for breakfast? How can you even stand up?"

His uncle grinned. "Wow! You can really hear her. That is so cool!"

Chapter Fifteen

"That's it," said Lux. "I'm tired of relaying messages from Umbra. Just because I can talk to her doesn't mean I want to be her personal speaker."

"All hail the speaker of the girl." Spinnet bowed and his pillbox hat rolled across the floor.

As Leeward chased down his hat, Lux picked up the saucer with the invisibility charm. Paper-thin leather wrapped around something lumpy, a black cord tied the edges together.

"Lux, put that down!" said his mother.

He dropped the pouch back onto the saucer. "What's in that thing? How does it work?"

"The pouch is made from lizard skin, and inside I think you would find three nutshells of Wolf's Bane seeds, which were gathered just after midnight of a full moon," said Cerri. "It's a classic invisibility charm."

"And Mr. Spinnet made that for Umbra?" he asked.

'Yes,' Umbra replied in his head.

Lux smiled. "Oh yeah! I forgot I could just ask you!"

"That reminds me," said Aunt Sophia. "We were going to ask Umbra how she knew about the coming of Murklin and the bodkin."

Lux sighed. "Here we go again."

Umbra related her answer to Lux.

"She heard herself say it," he said.

"She said it?" asked Cerri. "To herself?"

After a moment, Lux said, "A voice told her to talk to Mr. Spinnet about making an invisibility charm because the traitor was coming with the spike. She didn't know it was her voice until later."

Atlas threw up his hands. "Well, that clears everything right up. Sort of." He grinned at Umbra. "I'm so glad to see you back to normal. Why don't you kids go find some trouble to get into? We'll take care of the dishes this morning."

"Sweet!" said Lux.

Umbra followed him out the door. They stopped in the hallway and heard the unfamiliar sound of a lock clicking into place. Lux tried the door behind them.

"Whoa. They locked us out," he said.

Umbra shrugged. 'Let's explore!'

Lux stared at the door for a moment. 'Yeah, okay. Go get your flashlight,' he said. 'I'll get that lock picking set Crowley gave me for Christmas and meet you in the rotunda.'

'Take a map.' Spinnet's voice rang in their heads. 'All adventurers need a good map.'

'We don't have a map,' Lux replied. 'Does Aunt Sophia have one somewhere?'

'Of course not,' he said. 'Who needs a map of their own house?'

Lux looked at Umbra, at a loss as to what to say.

'Do you have a map, Mr. Spinnet?' she asked.

'Certainly,' he said.

'Cool,' said Lux. 'Can we borrow it?'

'Borrow what?' Spinnet asked.

Lux rolled his eyes. 'Can we borrow your map?'

'Of course,' said Spinnet. 'Which map do you want?'

Umbra giggled. 'We want the one of Aunt Sophia's house.'

'How fortuitous,' he said. 'I happen to have it right here in my hat.' Spinnet's heavy steps crossed the kitchen and a folded piece of paper sailed under the door.

'Thank you, Mr. Spinnet,' said Umbra.

'Yeah, thanks,' added Lux. He unfolded the map.

'It was a pleasure to serve you,' Spinnet replied.

Lux grinned at Umbra. "Ready?"

It took a while to decipher the map. It looked to be a floor plan of Six Mile Farm, but unlike any

155

plan they'd ever seen. The footprint of the house was obvious. Two black lines denoted the thick exterior walls. Crossing those lines, a network of wide red paths intersected under the house.

'Maybe those are ley lines,' said Umbra

'Yeah,' said Lux. 'Didn't Aunt Sophia say the store was built over a bunch of ley lines? John Pickingill probably built his house over an intersection too.' Lux pointed to the other lines. "But what about all those? What the heck are they?"

Hundreds of thinner lines criss-crossed the page: black, green, red, blue, dashed, solid, dotted and lettered. The result looked like a dozen different colored spider webs lay across the sheet. After a while, they realized the lines shown in short red dashes reflected the main floor plan of the house; the ones shown in long red dashes indicated the basement floor. The lines made up of red dots outlined the second floor. What the other lines represented, they didn't know.

Lux and Umbra followed the red lines and ventured down hallways and into rooms they'd never seen before. They found Crowley's room, tucked up in the attic, his bed unmade and clothes strewn all over. They found Aunt Sophia's sunlight-filled room, though not in the same location they remembered from last year. They even found Aunt Sophia's root cellar, where she kept her canned vegetables, jams and fruits, as well as bottles of her homemade wine.

'Wow,' said Lux. 'I bet Crowley would pay a lot of money for directions to Aunt Sophia's wine cellar!'

Umbra nodded. 'He's been trying to find it for years.'

'We'll be rich!' Looking at the map, Lux realized with a chuckle that the wine cellar sat right under Crowley's own room, just two floors down. "Talk about something being right under your nose."

Around noon, their stomachs growled. They decided to head back to the kitchen. Lux tapped the map. 'We're right under the kitchen now, but to get to it, we have to take this passage that goes all the way out by the sunroom. That'll take forever.'

'There's got to be a shorter way," said Umbra. 'What about that?' She pointed to a narrow square on the map, hatched in red.

"What is it?" Lux forgot he didn't have to speak for Umbra to hear him.

'I don't know,' she answered, 'but it goes right to the kitchen.'

"You're right, Um." The square appeared to be embedded in one of the basement walls right under the kitchen.

'Secret stairway?' she asked.

Lux walked toward the section of stone and ran his hands over it. Umbra shined her flashlight over the wall. Her beam caught a pattern of shadows Lux hadn't noticed before.

'What is it?' Umbra asked.

157

"A ladder!" said Lux. His voice echoed through the stone corridor.

'Sh!'

'See how they carved these little slots in the wall?' said Lux. 'They're toe holds. And those rings on the sides, those are to grab on to. Cool. It *is* a secret stairway!'

They tucked the flashlight and map into their pockets.

"I'll go first." Lux climbed, pulling against the rings to keep his balance. About nine feet up, he crawled through a hole in the ceiling and bumped his head. Feeling around, he pulled himself sideways onto a small wood platform. The space measured a couple feet in each direction and just a few feet tall. He felt the wood walls, pushing and prodding.

As he pushed, the left partition sprang open with a metallic click. In the dim light, Lux saw neat stacks of pots and pans.

'Umbra, it worked! I'm in the kitchen cabinet.'

She crept up the ladder and crouched on the platform behind him. They heard a rumble of voices. Lux pushed the cabinet door open a tiny bit so they could hear better.

"I give up," said Atlas. "It sounds like a clear case of clairvoyance, but Umbra, being a St. Clare, should not have that gift. Of course, she's already shown a talent for foretelling, which she also should not have. And now we have Lux's gift of telepathy to top it all off."

"Technically," Cerri put in, "telepathy is not considered a gift. Many wicces have that ability."

"But not wiccas. It's very rare for a male to be gifted with telepathy," Aunt Sophia said. "In fact, the only other man I know who has that ability is Leeward."

"And Ambrose Murklin," added Atlas.

"Did someone call me?" Spinnet asked.

"No dear," Aunt Sophia said. "I agree with you, Atlas. Something very strange is going on here, and I am at a loss to come up with any explanation-- save one."

"But that's crazy," Cerri cried. "It's just not possible. I mean, why them?"

'They're talking about the Two again,' said Umbra. 'What does that mean?'

Lux repeated the Legend of the Two that Crowley told him.

"Calm down, Cerri," said Atlas. "I know it's hard to imagine our own kids being—well, legendary, but Legend of the Two has been fulfilled before, many times actually. You know that as well as I do."

"I'm not saying I don't believe in them," she said. "I'm saying I don't believe it's *them*."

'So,' Umbra said. 'They think we're the Two?'

'No,' said Lux. 'They think you're one of the Two.'

"It is possible," countered Aunt Sophia. "It's entirely possible. Besides, what other explanation would you give us?"

"I don't know," said Cerri. "But I just can't believe my own flesh and blood... the fulfillment of a legend?"

Umbra tugged his sleeve. 'What about your telepathy?' she asked. 'That's a gift, and you're not supposed to have anything but mind control.'

Lux thought for a moment. 'That's different. Mom said telepathy isn't considered a gift.'

'Not with girls, but AnSo said boys hardly ever have it.'

Lux considered that. 'No way, Umbra. It's too crazy.'

The phone rang and Crowley answered it.

"Sure--hang on a sec," he said. "Atlas, the phone's for you. It's Beatrice from your office."

Footsteps crossed the kitchen and Atlas said, "Hello Beatrice!"

Spinnet hummed Camptown Races while Aunt Sophia cleaned up the dishes.

"Yes, yes, of course," said Atlas. He sounded strange, sort of choked up. A chair scraped the floor and more footsteps crossed the kitchen.

"What's wrong?" Cerri asked.

"Thank you for calling," said Atlas. "I appreciate that, Beatrice. Goodbye"

"What was that all about?" said Cerri. "You're white as a sheet."

"That was Beatrice calling with a message from my Aunt Francesca. There was an accident this morning. Her son, Benedict, was killed."

160

"Oh, dear," said Aunt Sophia. "I'm so sorry."

Umbra whispered in Lux's head. 'Who's Benedict?'

'One of Dad's cousins. I met him once,' said Lux. 'You were too little to remember.'

The kitchen remained so quiet, he and Umbra dared not move. Lux's legs cramped as the seconds ticked by.

"Atlas?" said Cerri. "What's going on?"

His dad sighed. "If everyone could please sit down, there are some things I have to tell you."

"I don't like the sound of that," Cerri said.

"I'm not sure where to begin," said Atlas. He paced around the kitchen, coming very close to Lux and Umbra's cabinet. "Truly, I had hoped I would never have to tell you these things. But with Benedict gone..." He lapsed into silence.

"Whatever it is, just tell us," said Aunt Sophia.

"Right," said Atlas. "First, you need to understand that what I'm about to tell you can never be repeated. Ever. You'll understand why soon enough." He took a deep breath.

"My family, like many other Wiccae familes, has a prestigious lineage. The St. Clares were one of the original five craft families. Many noble and renowned names appear in my family tree. But the St. Clares were not exclusive in their marriages, and many not-so-famous names are woven into the tapestry. This fact makes the other branches of my ancestry very hard to trace.

161

"One of those branches runs back, hundreds of years, to a family named "Spratt". They were of the Wiccae, farmers and blacksmiths mostly. They possessed no great wealth, nor any remarkable power. The Spratt's of the Dark Ages were a typical, hardworking Wiccae family. Except for one thing.

"They had been, since beyond memory, the keepers of a box of ruby-handled tools."

"Wait, do you mean... Are you seriously talking about the Rutilus Sardonyx?" Cerri asked.

'The Red Tools!' Lux said.

"Yes," said Atlas. "The tools were passed down through the family from mother to son, and father to daughter. Always male to female and vice versa. If there was not a family member of the opposite gender in the immediate family, then one was chosen from among cousins, nieces or nephews. That tradition has continued to this day.

"No one knows exactly who has the tools at any given time. Even within the family, the caretaker's identity remains hidden. That strategy has protected the tools through the years. We know that the Spratt secret has been compromised at times, but we don't know who may have kept tabs on it carefully enough to determine who holds the tools now. The family knows the tools could reside with either my Aunt Francesca or Aunt Mathilde. Even I don't know which one is the caretaker. So, the tools are safe...for now."

Lux sat in the dark, his hand over his open mouth.

At last, Aunt Sophia spoke. "What do you mean 'safe for now'?"

"Mathilde had a son," said Atlas. "My cousin, Mitchell, to whom she could pass the tools. And Aunt Francesca had Benedict to take them. Likewise, my mother had me. So, when the caretaker died, the tools would have passed directly to her son, but no one would have known if it was Mitchell or Benedict or me. Does everyone follow?"

"Yes, but that doesn't answer my question," replied Aunt Sophia. "And why have you chosen to share this with us? It seems as though this information is not typically discussed, even within the family."

"I tell you because now, this affects every one of you," he said.

"How is that?" Cerri asked. Her voice had a wary edge to it.

"Unfortunately, Mitchell died several years ago. And now, Benedict is dead, too. That means, regardless of whether Mathilde or Francesca has the tools, there is only one person to inherit them when the time comes. Me."

"I knew it was you," said Spinnet. "You're my favorite of them all."

"Oh dear," muttered Aunt Sophia.

'Too cool,' said Lux. 'Our own dad! The keeper of the most famous of the Tools of Legend!'

163

'And someday, they'll pass to me.' Umbra sounded as concerned as Cerri.

'You're not happy about that?' he asked.

'No!'

'Why not? Why does everyone sound so scared?'

Umbra just shook her head.

"I still don't understand how you getting the tools affects all of us," said Crowley.

"The tools have been sought after, by both Wiccaens and non-Wiccaens. You can imagine what kind of reward would be paid for them by someone like Sprenger. That means, whoever holds the tools is in a fair amount of danger. The only thing that's protected the caretaker in the past is that no one knew, for sure, who the caretaker was. But once my aunts pass away, it's going to be obvious to anyone keeping track that...it's me."

Lux formed a silent 'o' with his mouth. *Anyone keeping track...gee, I wonder who that might be. Maybe, the MM?*

"If someone did know you had the tools, what would they do?" asked Cerri.

"I don't know," said Atlas. "Chances are no one has been able to keep track of the lineage over eight hundred years. It would have been a difficult task. And if that's the case, then nothing will happen."

'And if it's not the case?' Lux wondered.

Umbra took his hand and held it in the dark.

* ***** *

Far away from Six-Mile Farm, in a stark white office, overlooking the city of London, a tall man with a hooked nose sat at a carved mahogany desk. He put his tea cup on a silver tray as a tap sounded at the door.

"Come in," he said.

A small man wearing an elegant grey suit stepped into the room. "Sir."

"Yes, Hitchings," said the man. "You have news?"

"Yes sir. We've just heard from one of the American agents. Benedict St. Clare has been killed this morning while skiing."

The man with the hooked nose pushed back from his tea, eyebrows raised. Making a tent of his fingers, he rested his chin on them and heaved a long sigh.

"Excellent," he said.

Amy Allgeyer Cook lives in Boise, Idaho with her husband and son, two ducks, one chicken and a feral house cat. She runs her own architecture firm and enjoys writing books, playing soccer and eating cupcakes.

Learn more about her, Lux and Umbra and Book Two of the Sardonyx Trilogy at:
http://www.The IronBodkin.com

Made in the USA
Lexington, KY
16 September 2010